Urgent C
Pumpkinfest

A Travel Writer Cozy Mystery #2

By Kelly Young

Enjoy!
Kelly Young

Table of Contents

Author's Note

Please be aware that this book uses Canadian spelling. Not because I am incapable of using American spelling, but because I am too attached to my extra u's and my zeds. You can pry my superfluous u's from my cold, dead keyboard.

You are intelligent people. I'm sure you can handle it.

Throughout the story, you will see the characters enjoying various pumpkin based treats. At the end of the book, you will find recipes for the treats mentioned. I wanted to do something that took into account the pumpkins at the heart of Pumpkinfest, so I sent out a call to family and friends. They came back with some really interesting recipes. My niece, in fact, invented one just because I suggested it! I hope you enjoy them.

The photo on the cover was taken by yours truly. It is not, however, of a location in Port Elgin. Rather, it is of a lovely pumpkin display at Sarah's Farm Market on Sandy's Street in Chatham, Ontario.

Also, while the town of Port Elgin, some locations within it, and certain characters are very real, I have taken liberties and artistic licence with some aspects of life in the small town to make the story flow better. My apologies to any Port Elgin folks who might take offence, as none is intended.

Dedication

For all of the people out there who demand pumpkin spice everything. I personally think you are a little bit crazy, but to each their own. This book likely wouldn't exist if it weren't for all of you.

Acknowledgements

This book could not have happened without the help and patience of a number of people.

- Ilene Scott, for playing tour guide and serving as my research consultant. Check out this very talented artist at https://www.shorelineartists.net/ilene-scott.html.
- Lynn Brown, my editor, for her hard work. I know I've told the joke correctly when she writes BAAAAAHAHAHAHAHAHAAA in her notes.
- Samantha McIsaac, for her advice on medical questions.
- Bonney Green and Deb Hawrylyshyn, for volunteering to be a Beta reader.
- All of the wonderful Cozy Mystery writers in whose books I immersed myself for inspiration.

Recurring Cast of Characters

The following is a list of recurring characters in the Travel Writer/Travel Writer Day Trips cozy mystery series, the books in which they appear, and a brief description of each.

The Piper Sniper (PS), *Urgent Quest at Pumpkinfest* (UQP), *Christmas Tree Mystery* (CTM), *Lethal Shot on Flowerpot* (LSF), *Wine and Whines* (WW)

Casey Robertson - PS/UQP/CTM/LSF/WW

A former reporter, now retired, and a current photojournalist for *Our Ontario* magazine, she has a reputation for being a klutz, and a notoriously picky eater.

Jim Robertson - PS/UQP/CTM/LSF/WW

A retired engineer and Casey's husband, he is a constant and patient presence.

Ed Wolsey - PS/UQP/CTM/LSF/WW

He is a retired police detective, an unapologetic slob and bear of a man, is known for having a short fuse, and has a checkered history with Casey.

Myrna Holmberg - PS/UQP/CTM/LSF/WW

A Kincardine resident in her seventies with a mysterious past that intrigues Casey. She has prior experience as a medic, carries an enormous handbag with all sorts of surprising things inside, and is best friends with Ilene Anderson.

Ilene Anderson - UQP/CTM/LSF/WW

An old friend of Myrna's, owner of *Mariner's Rest B&B* and the *Port in a Storm Cafe* in Port Elgin, she shares the same mysterious past with her friend. She was possibly a lawyer earlier in life.

THE TRAVELLING KLUTZ

My name is Casey Robertson, and I am the photo journalist responsible for The Travelling Klutz feature in Our Ontario Magazine. I travel to small towns in Ontario, Canada and highlight the towns' unique features for my readers, in hopes that my articles will encourage the readers to also visit some day.

The column is a new addition to the glossy, bi-monthly magazine, and I am starting my feature by writing about some of my own favourite Ontario small towns. To date, I have completed one article, focussing on the town of Kincardine, nestled on the shores of Lake Huron. The article was a success with readers and the magazine has given me the go ahead for more.

So I am now turning my attention to the small town of Port Elgin, Ontario. Also, on the shores of Lake Huron, Port Elgin will be hosting me and Jim, my handsome hubby of 34 years, during the largest event on its calendar - Pumpkinfest.

One can only hope that this assignment goes better than the last one did.

But you know what they say. "The best laid plans..."

Chapter 1

"Oh please, let us have one of the turret rooms!" I stared up at the stately Victorian house before me, stunned by the sheer grandeur of the building.

The majestic building stood three stories tall, on the corner of Green and Harbour streets, overlooking the blue vista that is Lake Huron, one of North America's Great Lakes. The old home had pale yellow siding and white trim, with an eight-sided turret on the west side, its roof culminating in a peak that reached high into the sky. On the second floor, beside the turret and above the entry way, just visible from the street, was a small, private balcony with simple white furniture. A wide veranda wrapped around the house, with white wooden rocking chairs positioned strategically, perfect for enjoying an evening beverage with friends. A set of wide stairs leading to the entrance divided colourful gardens that ran along the base of the building, and the entire front lawn was surrounded by a decorative black, cast-iron fence.

"I don't know, my sweet," my husband Jim commented as he dropped our bags on the sidewalk beside me. People have often said that he resembles an older Kevin Costner, but all I know is that he is devilishly handsome, with his now full head of grey hair and laugh lines that give his eyes an extra warm look. The fact that he is taller than my five foot ten is just a bonus.

I had been in such a rush to get a better look at the Bed and Breakfast that would be our base of operations for the next few days that I had left him to deal with our belongings on his own. "Those rooms may be a bit small," he observed.

I turned and smiled up at him mischievously, tossing my short wavy hair out of my eyes; in my 55th year it was just starting to show signs of grey in the dark blonde. "I'm sure I can fit into one nicely," I teased, as I wiped the sweat from my brow. It was unseasonably hot and humid for the first week of October. It was so hot that I was wearing my favourite tank top and shorts that were usually shoved to the back of the closet by this time of year. Regardless what room we ended up in, I fervently hoped the bed and breakfast had air conditioning. I couldn't remember the last time I'd worn summer clothes this late in the season. "You can stay somewhere else if it's too small for both of us," I added.

He raised a perspiring eyebrow in an impressive Spock impression - the Star Trek one, not the doctor - and was about to reply, but was interrupted before he could speak.

"The invitation to stay with us still stands," a familiar female voice spoke from behind us.

I spun around and let out a squeal of delight at the sight of Marie Battler, my old friend, colleague, and boss. "You made it!" I exclaimed. In my rush to give her a hug, I crashed into the bags that Jim had just set down. Both bags tilted on their wheels and I tilted as well, without the excuse of wheels for my imbalance. Jim was left having to quickly decide between rescuing our bags and preventing me from tumbling over them.

He reached out and grasped my elbow firmly, letting out a long-suffering sigh as he watched both of our bags tumble to the ground like the beginning of a domino line.

I knew that I had married a smart man.

I smiled sweetly as he muttered something unintelligible under his breath, then I turned to give Marie the intended hug. I swear I could almost feel her roll her eyes as she hugged me back.

"Of course, I made it. I only had a 15-minute drive," she groused. "Seriously Jim," she addressed my husband over my shoulder, "if you finally want some time away from this crazy klutz, you can come back home to Tiverton with me. You know Will would be glad to have you visit."

Jim chuckled in response. "I would be perfectly happy sharing the tiniest of rooms this inn has with Casey," he told her. "As long as we're together."

"Ya, ya, ya," Marie scoffed. "One of these days you'll get over this nauseating lovey-dovey stuff." Her brown eyes twinkled merrily. "I just hope that I'm there to see it."

I smiled at the old, familiar banter as I turned to admire the B&B again. "Would you look at this place!" I exclaimed, a touch of awe sneaking into my voice. "It's like something out of a storybook."

She squinted her eyes and brushed her dark bangs aside as she looked up at the pristine building. "You had better hope that place is air conditioned. I had half a mind to turn back and head home, just so I could stay in the nice cool car." She fluffed out her tank top in an attempt to get some cool air against her skin. "But you're right about the B&B. It has you written all over it."

While Jim righted our luggage, the two of us stared up at the building. Located as it was on a side street that came off Highway 21, the thoroughfare that neatly dissected the town in two, the B&B would provide us with a central home base for the five days we were visiting.

Jim looked at the two of us for a second and shook his head ruefully. "You'd think the two of you hadn't seen each other for ages," he teased.

We both frowned at him.

"It HAS been ages!" I informed him.

"It's been three months," he countered.

"You say that as though three months is a short time," Marie accused him.

A lifted eyebrow was his only response.

"Besides," I added, "we weren't sure she could get the time off." I turned to her. "How DID you get the time off?"

Marie was the long-time editor and main reporter of the Kincardine newspaper, a half hour drive to the south.

"I didn't," she answered. She pointed behind me. "Look how lovely the B&B's sign is."

"Oh no you don't," I said in alarm. "You are not distracting me. What do you mean, you didn't get the time off?"

Marie rolled her eyes again. "Just what I said. I'm working this weekend."

"But you can't be!"

"Why not? You are."

She had a point there. We had timed our visit for the busiest time in the town's tourist season - Pumpkinfest, traditionally held on the weekend before Thanksgiving. It had seemed like an ideal time frame in which to write my second article for the Travelling Klutz feature in Our Ontario Magazine.

We had booked the bed and breakfast only a few weeks before, the need to do so having slipped our minds after our misadventures further south along Lake Huron's shores in Kincardine. We had become entangled in a mystery involving the murder of a member of the Kincardine Scottish Pipe Band, and the attempted murder of another. The jealousy-fueled woman at the core of the events had very nearly ended my life as well.

I really hoped this article would have a bit less excitement involved in the research phase. After all, I was getting a bit too old for such shenanigans.

Jim cleared his throat, drawing both of our attention to him. "So Marie, do you have to go back to Kincardine?"

She frowned at him. "I was going to torture her for a while longer," she groused.

"We only have five days here," he retorted dryly.

She chuckled, and then turned back to me. "I switched with the editor of the Port Elgin Schooner," she admitted. "We're part of the same company, as you might remember, and we thought a change of perspective could do both papers some good."

I squealed again and gave a little hop. I felt like a teenager getting together with her best friend. A 55-year-old teenager.

"That's great!" I exclaimed, slipping my arm through hers and turning towards the B&B. "Have you ever stayed here?"

"We live 15 minutes away ..."

"So that's a no?"

Jim sighed and picked up our bags. "I'll go check in," he mumbled. I thought I heard something about looking forward to getting inside where there was air conditioning, but chose to ignore it.

"See if we can get a turret room," I called after him.

He waved a hand in acknowledgement. I took a moment to admire his still fit profile, only to get a slap from my friend.

"Cut it out," she grumbled.

I snickered, and turned my attention to our accommodations. Set back from the road, the gorgeous yellow and white Victorian was surrounded by lush green lawn, almost too green for the time of year, and majestic maple trees that were in peak fall colours. The unseasonably warm weather had pushed back the coming of fall, and it promised to be an exceptional weekend as far as the weather was concerned.

The rest, of course, remained to be seen. I flashed back to our misadventures in Kincardine and shuddered.

"Would you look at that anchor?" I pointed at a huge boat anchor, presumably from a lake-faring vessel, which sat perched at the beginning of the walkway leading to the house. Above it swung a decorative sign made from the same shade of cast iron as the fence, declaring the Mariner's Rest Bed & Breakfast had no vacancies. Pumpkins, gourds, hay bales, and corn stalks lined the walkway that led to the stairway leading to the main entrance of the building. "Do you think it's real?"

"Likely," Marie answered. "The lake bottom is certainly littered with enough wrecks to pick from." She started up the walkway towards the house and I turned to follow. We only managed a few steps before I pulled her to a stop.

"Just look at that veranda!"

This close to the house I could see not only the rocking chairs I'd noticed earlier, but small cafe style tables, chairs, and even some swings on the porch, encouraging guests to sit awhile.

"I can see myself sitting with Jim and swinging there, drinking a nice glass of wine."

"Unfortunately, I can picture that too," Marie commented dryly.

But it was the three-storey turret, with its large windows looking out over the street and the lake, which had really captured my attention. I was already imagining myself sitting in a window seat, writing or reading as a cool, fall breeze blew through the open window, making the sheer curtains billow inwards. "Maybe we shouldn't get a room in the turret," I said. "We might never leave."

Marie grunted in mock disgust. "Spare me the details," she growled.

"I didn't mean ..." I stammered, feeling a blush creep into my cheeks.

"Uh huh," she teased. "You always mean that."

"I meant I could see me sitting in the window seat, reading or working..."

She waved, as though clearing the air of my weak explanation. "Whatever. I just hope it's as nice on the inside."

"Oh, you haven't seen anything yet!" a voice came from behind us.

In 1988 the Township of Saugeen as well as the towns of Port Elgin and Southampton were amalgamated into the Town of Saugeen Shores. Nevertheless, Port Elgin is still known by residents and visitors alike by its original name. The two larger centres, Port Elgin and Southampton, sit about five miles apart; one can drive between them on Highway 21, boat up the Saugeen River or the shore of Lake Huron, or cycle or walk the popular North Shore Trail and Saugeen Rail Trail that run between the two communities.

Even when it isn't Pumpkinfest season, there is plenty to see and do in the municipality. It boasts stunning coastline and a total of 12 Lake Huron beaches, wonderful shopping and restaurants, great hiking and cycling trails, boating, and water sports.

One fun thing to do is a walking tour to take in the architecture of the area. Points of interest include the Lakeview Hotel, built in 1871 and renamed the Royal Princess Lodge before becoming the Edelweiss Motel; The Queen's Hotel, built in 1890 of bricks from the local Barthold Smith brick plant; the Arlington Block, built in 1880 also of local bricks; and the stunning Port Elgin Library, one of the few Carnegie Libraries remaining in Ontario, built in 1908.

There are also a number of stately old houses, some of which have been repurposed into Bed & Breakfast Inns, that are a sight to behold and worth a tour in their own right.

If you choose to stay in one of these heritage buildings, you might be surprised by the people you meet. Or meet again, as the case may be.

Chapter 2

Marie and I both jumped in surprise and spun to see who had come up behind us so quietly. We found ourselves gaping at Mrs. Holmberg. For her part, the tall and thin septuagenarian with wispy shoulder length gray hair regarded us in amusement.

We should have known. On my last assignment, Jim and I had rented a cottage next door to the 70-something Kincardine woman. She had demonstrated an uncanny tendency to pop up suddenly and disappear just as quietly. I was still convinced she had been a ninja in a previous life. Or at least in her younger years.

I pushed down my surprise and gave her a warm hug.

"It is so nice to see you, Mrs. Holmberg," I told her sincerely.

Marie nodded at her somewhat curtly. She hadn't had the opportunity to get to know the woman as well as we had. "You shouldn't sneak up on people," she admonished. "You could have given us heart attacks."

"Pfft!" the older woman scoffed, waving her hand in dismissal. "You are far too young for coronaries." She turned her attention back to me. "You look well, dear."

I smiled at the compliment. "Thank you for pulling strings and getting us into this B&B," I said. "We really appreciate it."

Again the hand waved. "You are very welcome," she answered as she moved past us and headed towards the stairs. "Ilene is an old friend."

I wasn't sure who Ilene was, but if I had to guess, I had a feeling I was about to meet her inside. We fell in line behind Mrs. Holmberg. As we climbed the stairs I admired the massive wooden doors, currently closed to keep the heat and humidity out, and the air conditioning in. Then I admired the sight of my handsome hubby standing on this side of the check in counter. Beside him on the counter was a large tin sign, in the shape of a pumpkin, with a verse written on it. The sign read

Peter, Peter, Pumpkin eater

Had a wife but couldn't keep her.

He put her in a pumpkin shell

And there he kept her very well.

I smiled at what I was sure was going to be the first of many pumpkin references we would see during our stay, and then turned to Jim.

"Well handsome," I said as I slipped my arm through his, "did you find out which room we're in?"

I didn't hold out much hope, realistically, for a turret room. It was an insanely busy time of year for the town's accommodations after all.

Jim looked like the cat that ate the canary. "I did," he crowed.

"You will be in the top turret room," the woman behind the check-in desk stated. She was a tall, slim, regal woman in her mid-seventies, if I were to guess, with grey hair in a perfect short cut, and friendly eyes that were currently twinkling with amusement.

I just stared at her in surprise, speechless.

"This is my long-time friend Ilene Anderson," Mrs. Holmberg piped up from behind me. "She is the owner of this amazing establishment."

When I failed to come up with something to say, Jim nudged me in the side.

"How?" I asked, genuinely puzzled and rudely skipping the pleasantries. That prompted a nudge in my back from Mrs. Holmberg.

I came to my senses while Marie and Jim tried hard to not laugh. "I'm so sorry!" I apologized. "It's very nice to meet you, Mrs. Anderson."

"Just call me Ilene," she answered, taking my proffered hand and shaking it.

"Ilene," I repeated. I had heard that if you do that, you are less apt to forget a person's name. It hadn't worked for me so far, but I lived in hopeful anticipation. "How did we manage to get a turret room? We called so late in the season."

"That you did," Ilene answered in a slightly scolding tone. "And normally that would have made things difficult."

"Impossible, more like," Mrs. H added. "What were you thinking?"

I flushed, embarrassed. "Well, I wasn't, really."

Ilene waved her hand at me in a very familiar manner. "Regardless, your lack of organization was not an issue," she explained, "because Myrna made your reservations months ago."

I frowned, puzzled. "Who?" I looked at Jim and he looked just as confused.

"That would be me," Mrs. H said with a chuckle.

We all stared at her.

"You have a first name?"

Ilene gave an unladylike snort, attempting to hide it with a cough as she turned to get a key for us.

Mrs. Holmberg - Mrs. H - Myrna - ignored my blurted comment. "You said you were coming for Pumpkinfest. Ilene and I go way back..."

"You don't have to put it quite that way," Ilene complained.

"...so I called and got you the best room that same day."

I looked at Ilene. "Why didn't the person taking reservations tell us we already had one when we called."

Ilene smiled. "I thought it would be fun to see your reactions when you got here and found out," she said. "And it absolutely has been."

I turned back to Myrna, thinking how using the new - to us at least - name might take some getting used to. "But, wouldn't you prefer to have that room?" I asked.

"I always stay in one of the rooms on the main floor," she answered. "That way, I'm closer to Ilene."

"Always? How many times have you stayed here?"

She shrugged. "We're old friends."

Ilene cleared her throat in protest. "Again..."

Myrna waved her hand, just as Ilene had earlier. "Whatever."

Ilene shook her head. "So, here is your key," she told Jim as she handed the old fashioned key to him. "You are at the top of the stairs."

Jim took the key, looked at the bags and decided to hand the key to me. "Thank you so much." He turned to Myrna. "To both of you."

The three of us headed towards the stairs, admiring the lovely watercolour paintings of local scenes adorning the walls of the B&B as we went. A closer look at them revealed that they were the work of our hostess Ilene. I determined to find out if I could buy one to take home as a souvenir of our stay before we left.

We went up the wide oak staircase to the third floor. As we passed the second floor, a glimpse down the hallway showed more watercolours adorning the walls between the various doors to other rooms. I noticed that each door featured a name instead of a room number. As we reached our room, I saw that it was named Ariel, presumably after the famous mermaid. I excitedly opened the door to get the first look at our accommodations.

"Oh my! It's everything I imagined it would be!" I squealed, tearing into the room ahead of the others so quickly that they almost got locked out when the door nearly closed shut behind me.

The room was eight sided, with floor to ceiling windows on four of the walls. From those you could see the two streets that bordered the property, and the lake beyond the street to the west. Off to the north, if you leaned over a bit, you could see a bit of the harbour. One of the windows had a cozy window seat, covered with nautically themed throw pillows. One light blue throw cushion was decorated with the words 'Seas the Day' in white lettering.

The bottoms of the walls with no windows were covered with white wainscoting, a light tan colour adorning the wall above. Against the back wall, a large white bed afforded an excellent view of the windows and presumably a wonderful sunset each night. A small efficiency kitchen was located beside a door that led to a private bathroom, both perks I hadn't expected.

I guess it really is all in who you know.

"This is going to be perfect!" I exclaimed.

"I hope so," Jim replied.

I gave him a quick hug. "This time the assignment will go off without a hitch," I reassured him.

Marie, who was looking out the window at the view, snorted. "You just had to say that, didn't you?"

Port Elgin's Pumpkinfest began in 1986 with its first weigh off, but it wasn't until two years later that it became part of the World Pumpkin Federation and the name Port Elgin Pumpkinfest became official. The event, meant to bring people to town in the 'shoulder season', grew from 200 attendees in that first year to an estimated 60,000 visitors in recent years.

The entire town is now involved in the festivities. In addition to the International Weigh Off of pumpkins and gourds, the festival includes such fun events as a Friday night 'Pub Kin Crawl', a car show, live bands, a midway and kiddie carnival, a petting zoo, a craft show, a marketplace, an art show, and much more. There is truly something for everyone at Pumpkinfest.

Part of the fun in attending the event is watching the town gear up for the festival, with businesses and houses embracing the theme and decorating accordingly. It's worth a tour around town just to get a good look at the decorating efforts before the crowds arrive in full force. Pumpkins, of course, are front and centre in the decorating scheme, but you will also find adornments that would no doubt be carried over into Thanksgiving and Halloween celebrations, such as corn stalks and hay bales.

Usually, cool fall temperatures create the perfect setting as Pumpkinfest begins the Thanksgiving and Halloween season. When the weather is unseasonably warm, however, things just don't feel the same. Attending the event in sweltering heat is definitely not what you expect of an event titled Pumpkinfest.

Not to mention that hot temperatures can sometimes lead to hot tempers.

Chapter 3

We had just returned to the lobby of the B&B, on our way to explore the area when an older gentleman, who brought to mind Canadian actor William Shatner, entered through the front door, scowling at a sheet of paper he was carrying in his right hand.

"Andrew?" I asked incredulously, surprised to see the member of Kincardine's Romeo club - which stands for Really Old Men Eating Out - here at a B&B in Port Elgin.

"Andrew!" Myrna exclaimed from a hallway to the left of the check-in desk, clearly happy to see him. "You made it right on time."

Andrew waved the paper at her, ignoring pleasantries. "Have you seen this? Young people these days!

Myrna walked over to him and stood on her toes to give him a kiss on his cheek. I looked over at Jim to see if he was as shocked as I was at this show of affection. Not only was she greeting a man whom she had only become acquainted with this summer, as far as we knew, with a kiss, but she was doing an enviable version of en Pointe as well.

Andrew seemed to forget the page he was holding, which was surprising given how peeved he seemed by it a moment ago. He returned Myrna's kiss with gusto, leaving us gaping anew. Using the kiss as a distraction, Myrna plucked the paper from his hand and passed it off to Ilene, who had come out from behind the desk.

Ilene examined the page and it was only a few seconds before she chuckled at what she was reading. She held up the paper so we could see the poster printed on it. "I like this girl," she declared.

The poster had the word BEWARE emblazoned in capital letters across the top, centred over a photo of a roguish young man, smiling at the camera, revealing two attractive dimples. Below the photo were the words CHEATER and LIAR, leaving no doubt as to why the man was featured on a poster to begin with.

I moved in for a closer look and to read the fine print out loud.

"Pierre Citrouille should be avoided at all costs. DO NOT DATE THIS MAN! He will charm you with his French-Canadian accent, then cheat on you with your best friend, all while lying to you for weeks."

The poster concluded with the words 'HE CANNOT BE TRUSTED!' in a large font that matched the headline at the top. I read that out loud, but then had to squint to read the tiny letters that stated 'And it is not 6 inches either".

I was having trouble containing my laughter as I read the final line. "Please spread this warning!" Having read the entire thing, I allowed myself to dissolve into a hearty belly laugh.

"That is one angry woman," Andrew observed, clearly much more mellow about the entire thing since he'd had that scorcher of a kiss.

"That is harsh," Jim added. "She could ruin the guy's life with that."

"Like he did to her by cheating on her with her best friend?" I snapped at him, surprised at his reaction.

"I'm just saying," Jim clarified, "couldn't this be slander? Or libel?"

Andrew nodded. "These things are everywhere," he told us. "On telephone poles, fences, bulletin boards ..."

Ilene barked out a quick laugh before turning serious. "Not on MY fence, I hope."

Andrew shook his head. "I took this one down and told the young lady posting them everywhere to move along."

"My hero," Myrna answered, rewarding him with another kiss.

Marie, Jim, and I stared at them in shock.

"What?" she demanded. "Life moves pretty fast. If you don't stop and look around once in a while, you could miss it."

"Is that from the Dalai Lama?" Andrew asked.

She shook her head. "Better. Ferris Bueller."

We all laughed.

"Will wonders never cease," Jim mumbled.

Like Andrew had warned, we saw a number of the posters as we walked downtown.

"She spared no expense, I see," I commented. "I'd love to meet this genius."

"It seems mean to me," Jim countered.

I frowned up at him. "You just don't like seeing a woman get the upper hand."

"That is not true!" he protested. "I love it when you have the upper hand." He wiggled his eyebrows suggestively.

"Oh gross! Get a room!"

We turned to face Marie. I hadn't even noticed she wasn't with us until she returned. "Where did you get to?" I asked.

"I went down to the beach to see if I could find the poster ... uh, poster."

I snickered. "And?"

"No sign of her."

We continued to walk to the downtown area. When we got to the main street, a dog walker with five dogs of various sizes, pulling at their leashes, passed us. She was clearly having difficulty keeping her charges in check. Further along, a hot dog vendor was just setting up on the closed street, a bright red and white umbrella providing shade above his cart. We stopped by The American Hotel, one of the historic buildings on the main street which currently housed a store called Cathy's Flowers 'N Treasures. My attention was drawn by a massive mural across the street from the flower shop. It was one of many painted by popular landscape painter Allen Hilgendorf, who had specialized in giant murals throughout Ontario.

The mural's title, *The Bustling Community of Port Elgin, Late 1800's,* was featured on a red banner painted on the bottom centre of the mural. On the left side the mural featured an old red brick railway station with a horse and buggy parked beside it, a large black steam engine stopped on the tracks in front. Beside that scene and toward the top, was an idyllic water scene with people on a dock jutting out toward a sailboat, schooner, and steamer floating on the glassy water. Centred above the banner containing the title of the work, were four women in period costumes that formed a brass band, complete with two trumpets or bugles, a French horn, and a tuba, while a young boy sat by them holding up a sheet of music. To the right and above that scene was a gazebo on a beach, where children could be seen playing. A rural scene with a grey brick farmhouse, complete with barn and tall elevator, a maple tree in fall foliage, a dairy cow in pasture, and the mural was completed on the right with a depiction of the Port Elgin Boot and Shoe Store. Like all of the artist's murals, this one took me back in time.

Marie crossed the road to take some close-up photos of the artwork, while I took photos from where we stood at the side of the American Hotel, the grey walls of which curved around the corner. We barely registered the sound of a window opening above us.

Jim's surprised grunt did get my attention, however. I turned to look at him and barked out a surprised laugh.

Perched atop his head was a bright orange pumpkin hat.

"Where did you get that?" I stammered.

He glared at me and yanked it off his head. Then he turned to look up at the apartment above us.

"Hey! We're walking down here!" he yelled at a young woman in the window, inadvertently imitating a stereotypical New Yorker. I started to laugh again.

He threw the hat down and it came to a rest behind me, just as the woman yelled, "Look out below!"

A pile of clothing fluttered out the window and floated toward us. Just as I looked up, a pair of men's satin boxer shorts landed squarely on my face.

"Aargh!" I cried out, struggling to free myself of what I feared could very well be a man's soiled undergarments. My panic at the thought had me jumping about in a dance usually reserved for an errant spider, my arms and legs moving as if they had a will of their own.

"Casey, stop!" Jim yelled, just before I slipped on some silky material and fell.

In an unusual stroke of luck, the landing on my behind was broken by something soft and plush: I recognized it as the pumpkin hat Jim had been lucky enough to have land on him instead of underwear. My flailing arms struck a large sunflower lawn ornament I had been admiring earlier on display outside the store, and I felt a flash of guilt as I heard it crash down with a deafening metal on metal sound.

Things happened quickly then, but to me events seemed to progress in slow motion at the same time.

I managed to get the offending men's underwear off my face in time to see the hot dog cart teetering over the curb, where it had been knocked by the force of the apparently heavier than it looked sunflower crashing into it. I flicked the boxers away from

34

me in disgust, sending them straight at the hot dog vender in my haste to be free.

The man was no more enthused to have a stranger's underwear fly at him than I had been, and he jumped back in alarm. As more clothing fell from the sky in a leisurely rain of cloth, the man rammed into his hot dog cart and it completed its tumble off the curb, spilling its contents onto the street, all the while emitting an oddly appetizing odour.

An odour that, naturally, attracted the pack of dogs that had just gone by, dragging a harried looking woman along with it.

"Oh no," I heard Jim lament.

Then things sped back up again for me. The dogs dragged their walker halfway across the road before she surrendered to the inevitable, letting go of their leashes rather than fall and be dragged. The dogs bolted for the feast of wieners strewn across the pavement, knocking over the vendor, who had just regained his balance after escaping the flying boxer shorts. He opted to stay on the ground, sitting among a mound of discarded men's clothing and scattered wieners, watching his wares get devoured by a motley pack of dogs.

I had never seen anything like it. And that is saying a lot.

"What the bloody hell is going on here?" a voice boomed out from behind us.

I froze, and despite the stifling heat, an eerie chill ran up my spine.

I knew that voice.

"It's not my fault," I said instinctively as I turned to face the very last person I expected to see, and the only person who could make this experience any worse.

Port Elgin's bustling downtown has plenty of shops and restaurants to cater to any taste. With Highway 21 running right through on its way north to the popular Bruce Peninsula area and south to the border with the United States, the downtown of Port Elgin benefits from a constant, ever changing traffic flow of newcomers and residents alike.

The Farmers' Market, centrally located in the downtown area, is held every Wednesday during summer. It's the perfect place to get your fresh produce, browse the work of local artisans and treat yourself to a variety of delectable edibles. While you are downtown, be sure to take in the various heritage buildings, such as the Arlington Hotel and the Public Library. And top off your visit with time on a patio or inside one of the many restaurants and eateries.

The people of Port Elgin are friendly and welcoming, willing to dispense with directions and advice on where to go and what to do during your stay. You are sure to meet some interesting people here.

Of course, some can be more interesting than others.

Chapter 4

"What are you doing here?" my old nemesis, Detective Ed Wolsey demanded gruffly.

A large man, both in height and girth, Wolsey looked like he had taken his lightweight suit out of the laundry hamper for one more use. He wore his almost completely grey hair in a brush cut. He had a habit of running his hand over his hair, something I'd come to associate with his frequent high level of exasperation. Let's just say he was not known for his sunny disposition.

We had a history - Wolsey, Marie, and I - going back to the days when I had been a reporter and Marie had been my editor. Once, after an evening of partying on our part, a particular and unfortunate run-in with the law resulted in a strained relationship between the local press and the officer who was forced to deal with us. Suffice it to say that incident set the tone for future encounters.

More recently, we had run into Wolsey in Kincardine, when we had helped him solve the case of the Piper Sniper. Much to his chagrin, I might add. Things ended with a kind of truce, but I still wasn't thrilled to see him here, especially after being front and centre in what he would no doubt call 'another incident'.

"What are YOU doing here?" I countered, falling into the old habit of answering his questions with one of my own.

Wolsey growled deep in his chest, then turned to Jim for an answer. "Another so-called 'article'?" he asked, making air quotes as he said the last word.

"Hey!" I protested, even as Jim nodded. I swatted my entirely too cooperative husband for good measure.

"De-tec-tive! Imagine seeing you here!" Marie said dryly, having decided to join the reunion. We had started drawing out his title as we addressed him after he had informed us of his promotion when we first ran across him in Kincardine in the summer. We continued mostly because we could see that it irked him. "Why are you here?"

Wolsey sighed as he surveyed the chaotic scene. "I had time off, and thought I would get in some overtime doing some paid duty helping out here over Pumpkinfest." He looked over at me. "I forgot you would be here, clearly."

A stray t-shirt, which had been caught on a brick on the building's wall, fell loose and fluttered to the ground at his feet. He glared up at the window, where the young woman stared down at the mess she had created.

"You!" Wolsey yelled up at her. "Police! Come down here right now!"

She stared down for another moment; her eyes the size of frying pans, then nodded, disappearing into the building.

"In the meantime," he said, turning to us, "explain."

The three of us looked at each other, Marie and I with expressions of glee and Jim with trepidation.

"I was taking a picture of the mural..." I began, pointing it out in case he had somehow missed its existence.

"I was still across the street..." Marie added.

"Getting in my way."

"Sorry about that."

I shrugged. "Apology accepted."

"I was here minding my own business," Jim added, "Only to get a pumpkin dumped on my head."

The young woman appeared around the corner and stopped, listening from a safe distance behind Wolsey. She looked winded and I watched as she took a puff from an inhaler. She was average in height, with a pretty, heart shaped face and dark blonde hair pulled back into a ponytail. She didn't look like someone who would be manically tossing clothing out of a second story window onto a busy street, but I reasoned that you never know what people are truly capable of.

Wolsey didn't see her yet, and held up a hand to stop our chatter.

"A what in the head?" he asked Jim.

"Typical," I muttered to Marie. "Go with the guy first."

Marie snickered and earned a glare from the detective for her reaction.

For his part, Jim ignored us and answered the detective. "A pumpkin," he explained, pointing to the hat now squished on the pavement. "It came from above and landed on my head."

"Of course it did," Wolsey muttered. "At least it wasn't a real pumpkin."

"That would have hurt," Marie observed.

40

"And likely would have hit me, not Jim," I added.

Jim just shook his head. I noted, however, that he didn't argue the point.

"A bunch of clothing followed..." Marie continued.

"I DID shout a warning," the woman behind Wolsey called out in her defence, instantly regretting her outburst when the detective spun around to glare at her.

"I will get to you in a minute," he snarled, his large index finger pointing right at her, causing her to move back a step in response.

I sighed, feeling sorry for her. "All that did was make me look up," I snapped at her.

Marie chuckled. "Like that time you were taking photos at the baseball game..."

...and someone yelled 'heads up'..." I added.

"...and you got the ball right in the leg because you didn't move."

Jim cleared his throat. "Uh, ladies..." he said, nodding toward the detective, who was turning an impressive shade of red.

I nodded. "So anyway, true to form, I looked up..."

"And she got a pair of men's boxer shorts right in the face!" Marie added with a laugh.

I saw Wolsey's lips twitch before he regained his scowl. "Of course she did."

Marie continued to laugh.

"You are enjoying this too much," I grumbled at her, pinching her arm in retribution.

"Ouch!"

"You had it coming." I turned to Wolsey. "When I realized what had happened, I panicked. Those could have been...used boxers!"

I heard a chuckle escape from Jim's direction and swatted his arm to shut him up.

"Officer, I believe that constitutes assault," Jim deadpanned before picking up the tale. "So, she was jumping around like a crazy person, backed up, slipped on more clothes, then fell and landed on the pumpkin hat..."

"And I knocked over one of those really big lawn ornament things the flower store had out on display..."

"Which hit the hot dog cart..." Marie added.

"And the rest was out of our hands," Jim concluded.

Wolsey stared at us for so long, I felt the need to fill the silence. "I did get the boxers off my face."

The hot dog vendor chose that moment to make his presence known. "She threw them on me and pushed my cart off the curb," he accused, pointing at me.

42

"Technically, the lawn ornament knocked your cart to the curb," I protested. "I couldn't even see at the time. And then you pushed it the rest of the way."

"And my wieners spilled everywhere!" he concluded, ignoring me, and his own culpability, completely.

Which, in retrospect, was probably a good thing.

"That would be when the dogs got involved," Marie added, pointing to where the dog walker was trying to pull all of the animals away from what remained of the spilled food. "She had better get them away from there, or they will all be sick later," Marie observed.

The vendor glared at her. "There is nothing wrong with my food!" he yelled at her.

She raised both of her hands in the universal sign of trying to placate an angry person. "Of course not! It's just if they eat them ALL..."

We all turned to watch the dog walker struggle with the leashes. A few bystanders decided to step in to give her a helping hand, which she quickly accepted.

"Oh! And I got it all on video!" Marie added happily.

Five heads swivelled to look at her.

"You couldn't have said that before?" Wolsey snapped.

I suddenly got a strong sense of déjà vu.

Marie shrugged.

"What about my cart?" the vender, clearly upset, demanded. "This is one of the busiest times of the year, especially given the weather, and I've lost a full supply of food."

A uniformed officer stepped forward at a nod from Wolsey. "Go with this officer to the station and he will get your statement," Wolsey said. He turned to the young woman. "Now, miss..."

"It is Mrs. I am married. For now. It's Mrs. Citrouille," she corrected. "But just call me Cindy."

"Cindy!"

We all turned to see who had called her name and stared at the man whose photo was featured on all the posters plastered around town. He was handsome; there was no doubt about that. He also exuded an air of confidence, overly so, as though he was accustomed to getting everything he wanted. Now that I was seeing him in person, I noticed that he was impeccably groomed, from his perfect dark brown hair and manicured finger nails to his clearly expensive, designer shorts, button down shirt and name brand athletic shoes. If the items his wife had tossed out the window were as top end as the clothes he was wearing, it was no wonder he was upset.

Everything about him made me think that this was a man who had no trouble with the ladies. That is until now, apparently.

I glanced at Wolsey, who seemed to be regretting ever taking extra duty in Port Elgin right about now.

"I am NOT talking to you Pierre!" Cindy shrieked.

Marie, Jim and I stepped back to lean against the building and, like many other bystanders, settled in for a show.

"What have you done with my things?" he stammered in shock, looking at the discarded items on the sidewalk, and then looking at his wife. "Sweetheart, you don't want me to leave." His French-Canadian accent was fully apparent, and he seemed to be laying it on thick in an attempt to charm his angry wife.

It didn't seem to be working for him though. "Yes, I do," she yelled at him. "And you WILL go! The lease is in my name. Only my name. You. Are. Out."

He scooped up some items from the sidewalk, examining them franticly for damage. "Let me explain..." he began, although his attention only seemed to be a fraction on his wife and more on the condition of his discarded clothing.

I leaned forward and pointed to the satiny boxers he had just picked up. "Um, you wouldn't know if those were clean, would you?"

Both he and Cindy turned puzzled looks my way before resuming their heated discussion.

"Explain what?" she screamed. "That you slept with my best friend?"

"Nice try," Marie whispered to me.

"It wasn't like that..." Pierre whined. "Darling, it didn't mean anything. You are the one I love..."

Cindy bent over and picked up a rock, winding up to presumably throw it at him like a missile.

"Enough!" Wolsey boomed, startling everyone within a city block. His explosion had the added benefit of frightening the pack of dogs into retreating with their guardian. Cindy froze long enough for him to reach out and take the rock from her hand.

"You!" Wolsey pointed at Pierre. "Gather your... belongings and find another place to stay."

Pierre wasn't quite done, however. "It's my air conditioner," he told Cindy. "Why didn't you toss that out?"

"WE bought it together!" she yelled at him. "And you know I need it for my asthma!" To accentuate her point, she took another puff from her inhaler.

Wolsey glared them both into silence before turning to Marie. "You! Send me that video file."

Marie nodded, uncharacteristically cooperative. "I have your e-mail address."

Wolsey then turned to me and Jim. "You two! Try to stay out of trouble."

"Yes sir," Jim mumbled, nudging me. I nodded in what I hoped appeared to be a contrite manner.

The detective pointed to the dog walker. "You get these animals to wherever they belong."

She nodded, thanked the people who had helped her, and hurried down the street with her charges.

Finally, Wolsey turned to Cindy. "And you are coming to the station with me."

"For what?" she exclaimed.

"Disturbing the peace?" I suggested.

"Littering?" Marie added.

"Assault with soiled undergarments?" Jim suggested. We all dissolved into laughter.

"But he deserved it!" Cindy protested.

"In handcuffs if necessary," Wolsey growled.

She sighed in defeat and hung her head. As Wolsey led her away, he turned to glare in our direction again.

"I know, I know," I muttered. "Don't leave town."

THE TRAVELLING KLUTZ

People in Port Elgin and the surrounding area are positive about one thing - the sunsets along their part of Lake Huron's shores are the most beautiful in the world.

With so much shoreline available in Saugeen Shores, there is no shortage of places where you can watch the sun turn the sky brilliant shades of oranges, purples, and reds. The reflection of the colours off the waters of the lake only accentuates the beauty. Every night you will find visitors and residents alike down by the water, watching the sun set.

Among the popular places you can go to watch are Northshore Park, where you can stroll along the harbour path, take a load off on one of the lake view benches, or lounge on a blanket on the grass. Viewing the nightly spectacle is even more idyllic from aboard a boat, or while swimming in the crystal clear waters of the lake.

The shoreline between Port Elgin and Southampton has plenty of public access spots from which to view the sunset as well. The S.S. Trolley runs daily between the two towns from the end of June to September. During Pumpkinfest, it runs Friday evening from 7 p.m. to 2 a.m. for the annual Pub-Kin Crawl: it's a fun, safe way to sample all the brews offered by local establishments and to get Pumpkinfest off to a good start.

Of course, when going from pub to pub, you are likely to hear all sorts of news once the drinks start to flow.

Chapter 5

We all sat in air-conditioned bliss around a massive wood block farm table in the Mariner's kitchen. The Port in a Storm Cafe was only open for breakfast and lunch, but as we had an 'in' with the owner, we were being treated to a tasty, cold buffet style meal.

"I really wish I had been there to see it," Myrna said wistfully.

Marie helped herself to meat and cheese from a plentiful charcuterie tray. "Where were you anyway?"

Andrew cleared his throat. "Never mind that," he muttered. Myrna flushed and we stared at them in surprise.

"Potato salad?" Ilene offered a heaping bowl of the salad, practically shoving it under Jim's nose.

"Sure," he stammered, before I yanked it out of his hand.

"You don't even like potato salad."

"Sure I do," he protested.

I rolled my eyes and took a huge helping before passing it along. "Marie got video," I mentioned as a distraction from Andrew's earlier implication.

Marie opened her laptop and brought up the video. Soon everyone was laughing anew at the day's antics, all thoughts of septuagenarian trysts forgotten for the time being.

"So, what's on your agenda this evening?" Ilene asked after the meal was done, as she stood to clear away the leftovers.

I rose to help her, but she waved me back into my seat. "We're going down to the water to get some sunset pictures," I answered.

"What?" Jim asked. "Why? Just use one of the million other sunset pictures that you have."

I frowned at him. "Those are of Kincardine sunsets," I told him, stating what was to me obvious.

"So?"

Perhaps it was not so obvious after all. I heard Marie snort beside me and kicked her under the table. "I need some pictures of the Port Elgin sunset," I said in a tone usually reserved for explaining something to a toddler.

Jim shrugged and dipped a piece of flatbread into the pumpkin spice hummus that hadn't been cleared away yet. "Same lake, same sky. No one would know." He sprayed some crumbs as he spoke. "Excuse me! This is way better than I expected," he added.

I looked at him in shock. "Are you serious?"

He nodded, and we had to wait for him to swallow before he replied. "Yes! I wouldn't have thought pumpkin in hummus dip would be tasty, but it is."

Marie laughed and rose from the table, grabbing my arm in the process and saving Jim from a swat. "As much as I'd like to stay and watch the rare disagreement between the nearly perpetual love birds," she said, "I have to get home."

"What? You aren't going to go on the Pub-Kin Crawl?" I asked. "We're heading over to catch the trolley after I get my sunset photos."

She shook her head as she swept her equipment into her massive camera bag, and then snagged a piece of flatbread to try the dip herself. "He's right, this is good," she said. "Ilene, thank you for the hospitality. Myrna, Andrew," she paused. "Don't do anything I wouldn't do."

I groaned, eliciting more laughter.

"Well, you know the old poem, don't you?" Andrew asked.

We all looked at him quizzically. Unfortunately, we didn't see Myrna shaking her head, or we wouldn't have encouraged him.

"When the weather is hot and sticky," he began with a wiggle of his eyebrows and a wave of his hand toward the window and the hot weather beyond, "that's no time for dunking dickey."

Both Myrna and Ilene snickered at the shocked looks coming from both me and Marie.

Andrew was determined to finish his poem. "When the frost is on the pumpkin, THAT'S the time for dickey dunkin'."

Jim snorted, spewing coffee from his nose. I handed him a napkin.

"But," Myrna added, "thank heavens for air conditioning."

"Aaand on that note," Marie said, "I'm out of here. Jim," she paused for effect, "enjoy the sunset."

"You're very welcome," Ilene called to Marie as she made her exit. Still chuckling at Andrew's poetry, she turned to me. "You go ahead too, Casey. If you don't go soon, you will have to wait until tomorrow night for your photos."

I looked at my watch and gasped. "Look at the time!" I grabbed my camera in one hand and Jim's hand in the other. "Let's go!"

"I thought you didn't need..."

I stopped and leveled him with a cold stare.

He visibly weighed his options, and then shrugged. "Of course you need some pictures of the sunset from THIS waterfront," he mumbled.

"I knew you would come around."

After getting around a dozen photos of the sun in various stages of setting from a spot near the harbour, I put my camera away in triumph.

"These pictures are gorgeous with the moored sailboats highlighted by the setting sun," I enthused to Jim. "And they are nothing like the sunset pictures from Kincardine, I might add."

We headed for downtown, where we would catch the S.S. Trolley to the Outlaw Brew Co. in Southampton. I'd convinced Jim to try their Pumpkin Jack'd Ale, and wanted to get there before he changed his mind.

"I will never question your photography expertise again," he promised dryly.

I chuckled as we continued our walk to the trolley stop. As we passed people on the sidewalk, it didn't take long for us to realize that the shenanigans from earlier in the day were now the talk of the town.

One group of three young women was particularly loud, suggesting they had already been taking part in the Pub-Kin Crawl.

"Did she really throw out all of his clothes?" one woman asked incredulously. She had dark shoulder length hair with orange streaks throughout, presumably as a nod to Pumpkinfest. She shook her head in a way that had the setting sun highlight the streaks as she spoke.

"Not just his clothes," answered a tall, thin woman, dressed in a Bohemian style look. "She tossed out ALL of his stuff!"

"She's my hero," a third woman declared. She was shorter than the other two and seemed to have to jog to keep up with them. They didn't seem too concerned with her ability to keep up, and I thought that was kind of mean of them.

"He must have been pissed!" the woman with the orange hair said.

"I'm sure he was. You know how he would only buy the best of everything," the shorter woman said. "And he's not exactly known for keeping his cool."

We were now passing each other and Jim and I went single file to give them room.

"The police had to break it up..." the tall woman said.

"Again," added orange hair. "The creep doesn't seem to think that sleeping around warranted being tossed out on his..." She suddenly noticed us and left her sentence unfinished.

"Has anyone seen Cindy since she got back from talking to the cops?"

They continued walking further away from us and we could hear them continuing their conversation, although the words were no longer clear.

"I guess we're going to hear a lot about this tonight," I said to Jim as we reached the trolley stop just in time. We could see the trolley, a large red and black wheeled vehicle, presumably fashioned after an electric trolley one would see in the south, approaching. When it stopped, we waited for passengers to stumble off before boarding the vehicle.

Once on board the trolley, we overheard variations of the same conversation as we headed toward Southampton. One group of young men chose to focus on the police presence at the incident.

"Did you get a load of that detective?" one man asked. "He looked like he was wearing something HIS wife chucked out of a window."

Luckily, the laughter from his friends drowned out my own amused laugh. I'd have to remember to pass that one on to Marie later.

"I didn't even know clothes came in double extra jumbo," another man mocked, getting more drunken guffaws in response.

"Now that's just mean," Jim leaned over and whispered in my ear. When I laughed, he shook his head at me. "You are supposed to be a grown up," he admonished.

"Maybe where the detective isn't concerned," I answered. "I have to remember to tell Marie this."

"Of course you do."

I looked out the trolley window, catching glimpses of the still brilliant sunset as we went. I held up my camera and took a few photos through the window.

"Those will probably be blurry," Jim opined.

I shrugged. "That's the beauty of digital," I told him. "No harm, no foul."

When we got to the pub, I took pictures of it inside and out, and followed up with pictures of its signature brew and pumpkin brew while I was at it. A mixed group of young people at a nearby table attracted my attention.

"Apparently, the video is online," one young man slurred.

Instantly, each person was holding a phone and searching for the video in question. When I heard my own voice come from the nearest phone, I shuddered and slunk down in my seat in hopes that none of the people at the table would recognize me.

56

"Don't worry, my sweet," Jim leaned over and told me. "They won't recognize you without underwear on your head." I kicked at him under our table, missing and stubbing my toe on the table leg and causing him to laugh harder.

"Hey!" a girl called over. "You're the guy who had the pumpkin hat land on his head."

It was my turn to laugh as Jim, embarrassed, simply nodded his head and turned away, taking a big swig of beer in the process.

The girl turned her attention back to the video, which everyone seemed to be watching at this point. Laughter filled the bar, overpowering any conversation that might be going on.

"Maybe we should proceed to another location," I suggested nervously, "before they recognize anyone else from that video."

Jim laughed. "Then drink up, buttercup." He pointed over to a man sitting at the bar. "Although I think we might be able to deflect attention onto him."

I turned and saw a dejected man sitting, drinking a pint of beer. After a moment I recognized the hot dog vendor.

"I feel kind of bad for him," I said.

"Well, you can run interference for him then," Jim suggested.

"I said I felt bad, but not that bad," I deadpanned. I drained the rest of my pint of beer. "Let's go!"

"You're all heart, my sweet," Jim said as he followed me out the door.

THE TRAVELLING KLUTZ

While the Friday night Pub-Kin Crawl is a great way to get in the spirit of Pumpkinfest, the event doesn't really take off until Saturday morning, with various affiliated events running all weekend.

The Port Elgin branch of the Royal Canadian Legion kicks things off with a delicious buffet breakfast, followed by the Business Improvement Area's Farmers' Market on Green Street. After picking up some great and tasty finds, head on over to the Shoreline Artists Show & Sale at the Community Complex, or dream about your next cool ride at the Motorcycle Show & Shine put on by the Grey Bruce Motorcycle Touring Club.

Those wanting to work off the extra calories they took in the night before can take part in a Mush Ball Tournament at the ball diamonds, or stroll through the Cinderella's Carriage Car Show. Take a break and watch a demonstration by the Grey Bruce Wood Turners Guild, then wrap up the day at the Lions Club Barbecue and taste the Rotary Club Official Pumpkin Pie. Or visit one of the many food trucks throughout the area for a delicious treat. In addition, there are events such as kids' pumpkin carving, chicken poop bingo, heritage activities, and educational displays.

You will be amazed at the giant pumpkin and vegetable displays: not only are the namesake pumpkins weighed, but other giant foodstuffs are in the competition as well. There are categories for giant squash, watermelon, cabbages, tomatoes, sunflowers, cucumbers, carrots and various different types of gourds as well.

Whatever you plan to do, make sure you start the day right with a good breakfast, be it at the buffet, your place of lodging, or at one of the many restaurants in town. While eating, you can plan out your day so that you don't miss a thing.

And if the day throws something unexpected at you, at least you will have the energy to deal with it.

Chapter 6

We started off the day a little worse for wear after sampling a number of seasonal brews during the Pub-Kin Crawl, so it was a more subdued group that convened in the Port in a Storm Cafe for breakfast. Jim and I strolled into the busy dining room to find that Myrna and Andrew had saved us spots at a large table.

"Good morning!" Ilene said more cheerfully than she had any right to be, in my humble opinion. She deposited a carafe of coffee on the table. "What's on the agenda for everyone today?"

"Coffee," I groaned, grabbing the carafe and pouring myself a cup.

"You say that like a zombie might say 'brains'," Andrew teased.

I filled Jim's cup and gave Andrew the stink eye. Deciding he didn't deserve an answer, I added milk to my cup and took my first sip with a sigh. It took a few moments for me to realize that my friends were waiting for an answer to Ilene's question. Since Jim didn't seem to want to jump in, I sighed.

"We'll be going down to take photos of the festivities," I muttered.

Ilene chuckled. "I have the ideal thing for that hangover, and it will get you through the day as well," she told me, mercifully speaking with a bit of a hush, before heading back to the kitchen.

Jim and I nursed our coffees, pouring seconds just before she returned with a tray containing four bowls.

"This is good for what ails you," she told us. "No matter what that might be," she added with a nod to Myrna and Andrew, who were whispering to each other like teenagers.

It was enough to give you a headache, assuming you didn't have a beer-induced one already.

I looked down at the bowl Ilene set before me. "Oatmeal?"

"Not just oatmeal," she explained. "Porridge and oats with protein. And a little something extra, of course."

"And that would be?" Jim asked.

"Why pumpkin, what else?" she laughed in answer.

"What else indeed."

She turned to leave, but I stopped her. "Ilene, one thing I haven't seen this time around is that giant pumpkin that used to be at the side of the highway on the north end of town as you head to Southampton. Do you remember it?"

She paused to think for a moment. "I DO remember it, but I haven't seen it in ages."

"Do you know where it went? I'd love to get a photo of it," I told her. "All those years of it being at the side of the highway and not once did I think to take a picture. I just assumed that it would always be there."

"I'm not sure where it is," she said. "But I will ask around and see what I can find out."

"Thanks, I appreciate it."

I took a tentative taste of the oatmeal. Ilene was right, it was really satisfying a craving I didn't know I had.

After the hearty breakfast, we headed downtown to check out the Pumpkinfest activities. The streets were rapidly filling with people enjoying the beautiful, though hot and humid day. The sun was beating down on us from an unobstructed blue sky and the heat already weighed heavily on us. We detoured a bit so that we approached the downtown area on Mill Street, which would allow us to stroll through the Cinderella's Carriage Car Show from end to end.

One of the largest two-day car shows in the province, it provided me with ample opportunity to photograph the classic, vintage and antique vehicles, as well as the people enjoying the show. I was taking a picture of a particularly pristine 1966 orange Ford Mustang with a white stripe centred over its hood, roof, and trunk when someone stepped into my frame. Irritated, I sighed and looked away from my camera screen to await a clear shot.

"Sorry," Marie said.

"You should be," I retorted, winking. "This is becoming a habit for you."

She opted against commenting. "You lost your shadow," she teased.

I moved my head to indicate the direction in which Jim had headed. "He saw a '67 Pontiac Parisienne down there. He just had to go over."

"Is it his dream car?"

"Ha! Hardly! His parents had one when he was a teenager," I explained, "and he insists that it tried to kill him."

"Really? What happened?"

"They got into a big pileup on Highway 11 in the snow, on their way up to the cottage. He got a pretty bad concussion."

"Well, that explains a few things."

I laughed. "No kidding, eh? Anyway, he's likely down there telling the owner to be careful with it. I think he believes they are all related to that car Christine from the Stephen King book."

"Do you think we should go rescue the poor person who has to listen to him?"

I shrugged. "In a few minutes. I don't want to ruin all of his fun."

"What fun is that now?" Jim asked from behind me.

I glared at Marie, who had seen him coming but hadn't given me a heads up. "The fun of telling strangers about your accident, way back when."

He turned to Marie. "Have I ever told you...?"

She quickly interrupted him before he could get into the tale. "Casey told me all about it."

I could tell that he was about to launch into the story anyway, but the orange Mustang caught his eye and he was instantly distracted. He looked at the woman who was clearly with the car and said, "Nice licence plate." His tone was dripping with sarcasm, and intrigued, I looked at the plate in question.

It was an Ohio plate, and it read 2 PUMPKEN. I snorted in surprise. Beside me, Marie took a moment longer to see the joke, but soon she was chuckling too.

Jim's sarcasm was lost on the woman with the car, however. "Thank you!" she beamed at him. "I got it for my husband as a Christmas gift last year."

The three of us stared at her, surprised that a wife would think that was a good license plate to give as a gift to put on her husband's dream car. She looked back at us, assuming she needed to explain her reasoning. "Because the car is pumpkin coloured," she said, sounding like she was pointing out something obvious to a five-year-old child. "And his name is Ken. So I just changed pump-kin to pump-Ken."

Jim was turning red from his clear effort to hold back his laughter. "And the number two?" he wheezed.

She shrugged. "The number one was taken."

"Oh my god!" Jim exploded into laughter. "Someone else has 1 PUMPKEN?"

The woman frowned at us. "I don't see what's so funny," she snapped.

I sighed, thinking if I sounded it out slowly, like I was speaking to a five-year-old, she might see what we saw. "One. Pump. Ken." I said, watching for the light to come on. When it didn't and she stared at me with an increasingly angry look, I added, "Your husband must be VERY secure in his masculinity to drive around with that license plate."

Marie and Jim broke out into a fresh round of belly laughs, accompanied by a few people who had overheard the conversation. In fact, a small crowd had gathered as the discussion had progressed. The sound of laughter was spreading. As we watched, our point finally dawned on the woman and she turned beet red.

"Oh no! That isn't what I meant at all!" she exclaimed.

"And your husband never mentioned it?" I asked, suddenly feeling sorry for her.

She shook her head, looking stunned. Mercifully, the laughter had died down in the face of her distress.

"Wow, I'd like to be around when you tell him," Marie chuckled.

"Our sons didn't say anything either," the woman muttered.

Jim did his best to stop laughing and wiped some tears from his eyes. "I think it was a very nice thought," he said, ignoring my involuntary snort of derision. "Clearly, your family doesn't have a dirty bone in your bodies."

I burst out laughing again. "Dirty bone! Really?"

It was Jim's turn to look surprised and embarrassed. "That was NOT what I meant, and you know it!" he said.

"I think we should just go," I suggested. "It was nice to meet you." I waved at the woman, grabbed both Jim's and Marie's arms, and made a hasty retreat. I was glad to see that the crowd was also dispersing.

"How could they not know?" Jim asked in wonder.

I giggled. "They know now."

We walked away from the pumpkin coloured car with the embarrassing licence plate, still chuckling. After about a block, we all got our giggles under control.

"I have some interesting current news," Marie said, looking like the cat that swallowed the canary.

We continued down the street and we both took photos as we talked. "Do tell!"

"Well, I ran into some young women who are friends with the jilted wife Cindy..."

"Did one of them have orange streaks in her hair?"

"You've met them?"

I shook my head. "No, we just overheard them talking last night. They were quite tipsy."

Jim chuckled. "Who wasn't?"

I ignored him. "So, what did they have to say?"

"They said that they can't find their friend!"

I stopped and looked at her. "They said they hadn't seen her last night either. But after that show she put on, I could understand her wanting to lay low."

Marie nodded. "That's what I said. But they don't think that she would do that." She paused for effect. "They think she has disappeared!"

"That's a bit of a leap," Jim observed.

I turned to get a picture of the brightly coloured cars lining the street behind us and saw the three girls in question. The orange streaks in the one girl's hair really stood out. "Speak of the devils."

The girl I had just noticed waved at Marie and they all hurried over.

"We went to the police, but they wouldn't listen to us," she blurted.

I stepped up to her. "Hi, I'm Casey and this is my husband Jim. I assume you've met Marie. And you are?"

She rolled her eyes at me and sighed. "Lori. This is Helen." She motioned to the tall girl. "And this is Velma." She waved a hand at the shorter girl who had just managed to catch up to her.

"And you are friends with Cindy?"

This time her eyes narrowed. "What's it to you?"

Marie stepped in. "Casey and Jim were instrumental in solving the Piper Sniper case in Kincardine this past summer," she said.

"I heard about that," Helen commented. She looked me up and down, as though sizing me up. "Didn't you get taken hostage?"

"Something like that," I muttered. I didn't like to remind Jim of the evening that I was taken hostage by an unbalanced woman and, but for the grace of my clumsy ways, almost shot. "I'm the one who had boxer shorts land on her yesterday," I offered up as a distraction.

The three girls giggled. I made a point of rolling my eyes at them.

"Well, you might be able to help then," Lori said. "We think Cindy has gone missing and the police won't listen to us."

"And why would you think that, exactly?" Jim asked.

"She was supposed to go on the pub crawl with us last night and didn't show," Velma answered quietly. We had to lean forward to hear her properly.

"So?" I asked.

"She would never stand us up!"

"You're going to need more than that to go on if you want the police or anyone else to take you seriously," Marie pointed out.

"Especially the detective currently in town," I added acerbically.

"That's why we're on our way to her apartment," Helen said. "There might be a clue to her whereabouts there."

Marie looked at me and I saw a twinkle in her eyes that I was certain was reflected in mine own.

"Want some company?" she asked.

"Oh boy, this ought to be interesting," Jim mumbled.

We followed the trio to Cindy's apartment above Cathy's Flowers 'N Treasures. We climbed the stairs to the apartment and Helen pulled out a key at the door.

"She gave me a key to look after her plants when they went on their honeymoon," she explained.

"When was that?" Marie asked.

"About six months ago," she answered. "Cindy told me to keep it because she and Pierre planned to travel a lot."

We entered the apartment and froze. The place looked like a tornado had ripped through. We had thought that all of Pierre's clothing had made it to the street to cause chaos, but the floor was littered with more men's clothing, mostly around the window looking out onto Mill Street. But more important was the condition of the rest of the living area we were currently surveying.

A large overstuffed arm chair had been knocked over and lay on its side. One lamp had been knocked off its end table and lay cracked on the floor. Fragile collectables were strewn, some broken into shards of porcelain and glass, across the floor near end tables. They looked like superhero figurines and, being a geek myself, I could imagine what the owner would think of having the collection trashed.

Velma gasped. "What happened here?" For the first time, I didn't have to struggle to hear her.

"It looks like there might have been a struggle," Marie stated, already taking photos of the scene.

"We had better not touch anything," Jim suggested.

"Why not?" Lori asked, clearly too dazed by the mess to think clearly.

"Because we have to call the police," I explained to her. "This doesn't look good."

She turned to look at me in surprise. "Is this something that the police will take seriously?"

My answer was interrupted by Helen. "Look! There's Cindy's purse!"

Jim frowned. "No woman would go somewhere without her purse," he stated.

"That's sexist!" Lori protested.

"Is it?" He looked pointedly at the three young women standing there, each with a purse over their shoulders, and then at me and Marie, both with camera bags in tow.

"He's got us there," Helen conceded.

"I'll tell you what she really wouldn't go anywhere without," Velma said ominously. "Those."

We looked to where she was pointing. On the kitchen counter in full view were her keys and the inhaler we had seen her use twice the day before.

"That's it," I said as I took my phone out of my bag, ignoring Jim's satisfied smile. "I'm calling our favourite detective."

Wolsey didn't seem too thrilled with the turn of events. We met him outside of the building and he immediately turned on Cindy's three friends.

"I told you three that failing to go out for a night of drinking does NOT mean your friend is missing," he growled.

The three of them visibly blanched. I felt bad for them. I remembered being cowed by Wolsey's attitude myself when I was younger.

"Get up on the wrong side of the bed this morning, Detec-tive?" I asked, running interference for the trio.

He narrowed his eyes at me. "What are you doing here?"

"I called you, remember?"

"These three don't need riling up," he informed me. "They are worked up enough as it is."

"With good reason," Marie told him. "Do you really think we would call you if we didn't think it was necessary?"

"It's not like we enjoy hanging out, after all," I pointed out.

Wolsey ran a hand over his head and sighed. "Fine. Why, exactly, did you call?"

"Cindy isn't here," Helen told him.

"Does she clear her whereabouts with you every day?" he countered.

"What she means to say," Lori added, "is that her apartment has been trashed."

That perked the detective up considerably. "And you know this how?"

Helen dangled her key in front of him. "I have the spare key," she said. "We let ourselves in." I was glad to see the young women had regained their footing and they were now standing up to him on their own.

"And not only is the place trashed," Velma said quietly, "but her purse, keys and inhaler are all still there."

"She wouldn't go anywhere without those," Lori told him, looking daggers at Jim briefly.

I snickered, getting a puzzled look from Wolsey and a quick nudge from my husband. I instantly regretted it, as I was once again on Wolsey's radar.

"And how did YOU three get in on this little excursion?" he demanded.

"They asked us to come along," I insisted.

"They didn't feel that YOU were taking them seriously," Marie added.

73

Wolsey's neck was turning red, a sure sign that we were irritating him. "There was nothing to TAKE seriously yesterday," he insisted, before changing tack. "Did you touch anything?"

"Once we realized what we were looking at, we came down here and called you," Jim said.

Wolsey nodded. "Still the voice of reason, I see," he told Jim.

I started to protest, but he pushed past me and held out his hand to Helen. "Keys!" he barked. She jumped and handed him her set of keys wordlessly. "We will look into this. You...six... go about your business."

"When will I get the keys back?" Helen asked.

"When we are done. We'll be in touch." As he headed to the door, I heard him grumble under his breath, "Now there are six of them. Wonderful. They're recruiting." And then, oddly, I could have sworn that I heard him add, "Well, two can play at that game."

THE TRAVELLING KLUTZ

One of the must-do activities when visiting Port Elgin is to cycle, or walk, the North Shore Trail.

The trail runs between the towns of Port Elgin and Southampton, along the stunning Lake Huron shoreline for a distance of six kilometres. It is perfect for cyclists, walkers, joggers, roller bladers, and skate boarders alike. Featuring a two-lane paved path and scenic lookouts, it is the perfect way to explore the shoreline; strategically placed benches situated along the route for rests or enjoyment of the views and lake breezes. Closer to Southampton, a wonderful view of the iconic Chantry Island Lighthouse awaits you.

Officially named the Chantry Island Lightstation Tower, the lighthouse was built of cut limestone and granite between 1855 and 1859. It is one of six Imperial Towers in Canada, built to guide sailors away from underwater shoals of massive granite boulders that wreaked havoc with navigation. The tower and keeper's house have been restored, offering limited tours of the facility to this day.

While on the trail, search the shoreline for beach glass and a wide variety of stones shaped by the relentless wave action. Take a quick dip into the cooling waters on a hot and humid day, although a day in October would not likely be ideal.

Or do both. You really never know what you will find when you look. Or even when you aren't looking.

Chapter 7

I needed some photos of the shoreline, so we decided to take a break from the Pumpkinfest crowds and the heat of downtown in favour of the cooler air afforded by the off-lake breezes along the North Shore Trail. We availed ourselves of the complimentary bicycles provided by the Mariner's Rest. Mine was a light blue cruiser with a wicker basket on the front and a wider, comfort seat, while Jim chose a dark blue men's version with a saddle bag frame on the back. Both were five speed bicycles, and we were certain that we wouldn't need more options than that on the fairly level trail. We loaded water bottles, snacks, and sunscreen into the basket, put some beach towels onto the frame on the back of Jim's bike, and donned our hats in preparation for a leisurely afternoon of cycling and taking photos.

We were surprised at the number of people down on the paved trail. We had expected it to be quiet, as it had seemed that the entire county was attending Pumpkinfest activities. We passed numerous other cyclists on the trail, as well as people out walking and roller blading. Many were enjoying the shoreline benches, taking in the view. The breeze off the lake was refreshing and despite the fact that we were exercising, we already felt much cooler than we had when we were downtown.

After about a half hour of leisurely cycling, interspersed with brief stops so that I could take a picture or more, we stopped for a rest in the shade of a tree adorned by brilliant fall foliage. I retrieved my water bottle from the basket at the front of the bike and took a long drink.

"Ah," I sighed. "Water is the absolute best."

"Better than wine?" Jim teased.

"Absolutely!" I surprised him with my unhesitating answer. "It's refreshing, whether you drink it or swim in it..."

"Beer is refreshing," Jim pointed out.

"But you wouldn't want to swim in it."

"That WOULD be an enormous waste," Jim agreed.

"You can drink water hot or cold, or make it even colder and freeze it for ice cubes," I continued.

"Which would come in handy right now," Jim observed as he drank the now lukewarm water from his own bottle.

"It turns to snow in the winter, which is so pretty."

"Until you have to shovel it."

"Touché. But even then, you can toboggan and skate on it."

"And likely get hurt, in your case, my sweet."

I threatened to toss the contents of my water bottle on him, but he just gave me a 'bring it' look. I decided that would be a waste of what amounted to liquid gold in this weather.

"And you can cook with it." I looked at him pointedly. "It's even an ingredient in wine and beer."

"Well, that convinces me then," he laughed. "Water is the most wonderful thing on the planet." He nodded down the trail, which ran closer to the water up ahead. "Shall we?"

I nodded, returned the water bottle to the basket, and pedalled after him down the trail. Ahead of us, we caught sight of the same dog walker who had been such a large part of the aftermath of the clothes throwing fiasco. One of her charges in particular, a Shi-Tzu, was barking at all of the bicycles as they passed by, straining against the leash in an attempt to give chase.

Of course, that got the rest of the dogs, four more in total, agitated as well. In a development we should have seen coming, the woman holding the leashes once again lost control of her charges. The Shi-Tzu took advantage of the dropped leashes and charged after the bicycles passing them at the time. The other four dogs, two of them on the massive side, charged after their miniature friend, their leashes tangling in the process and dragging behind them. We heard the woman yell "Oh no!" just before the entire circus charged in our direction.

I had only moments to react. And true to form, I reacted poorly. I swerved my bike to avoid catching the tiny dog in my wheels, causing me to career over the slope, a rocky divide, and right into the water.

Which was both a blessing and a curse.

As my engineer husband had told me a thousand times before: an object in motion will stay in motion, unless acted upon by an opposing force. The bike came to a sudden stop, catapulting me over the handlebars to splash down into Lake Huron. The bike had encountered an opposing force in the form of water. I had yet to do the same, and it didn't take long for me to follow suit.

I splashed down on my back in water about four feet deep. Luckily, on my flight over the handle bars, I flipped over far enough to protect my head, as we had opted to pass on the offered helmets. We hadn't thought we would need them during a leisurely ride on a cycling/walking path.

How wrong we were.

To add insult to injury, when they saw the splash that announced my entry into the water, the dogs lost interest in the bikes they had been chasing and turned to join me instead. Soon I was surrounded in the enthusiastic attentions of five dogs ranging in size from the tiny Shi-Tzu, who couldn't quite get to me because of the depth of the water, to what looked to be a large Newfoundland/Labrador cross. Thinking they were playing a game, the dogs splashed about, tangling me in the mess that was their leashes, and actually pushing me under the water a couple times.

Although the weather was unseasonably hot for October, the water had not received that particular memo: I was numb in moments.

Being soaking wet, freezing, and sore was, as far as I was concerned, the curse.

I tried to push the biggest dog off of me and looked up, expecting to see Jim ready to help. Imagine my surprise when I realized he was still on shore with about a dozen or so bystanders, looking at me in shock.

Luckily, the dog walker sprang into belated action. She called the dogs, which were suddenly much more willing to listen to her. I can only imagine that they had finally noticed the water temperature as well.

Once free of canine interference, and seeing that Jim had actually parked his bike and was coming to the shore, I put my hand down to push off the bottom and, hopefully, stand.

It was then that my hand came to rest on a hard, rectangular object.

I grabbed it and brought it with me as I stood. When I realized it was a cell phone, I knew it wouldn't likely work again, but I figured whoever had lost it would like to know that it had been found.

Jim was waiting on shore with one of our beach towels and, after making sure that all my limbs were still functional, I wasted no time getting out of the chilly water. I went to my husband and he wrapped the towel around me.

"Nice swan dive," he told me.

"At least I didn't hit my head."

He eyed my dripping shorts and tank top with a smile. "Still think water is the most wonderful thing in the world?"

I grinned, stopping when my teeth started to chatter. "At least it broke my fall. Without water, I'd have been seriously hurt."

That thought was a sobering one. I turned to the dog walker. "We have to stop meeting like this," I told her, a bit of anger leaking into my tone.

"I am so sorry," she shot over her shoulder as the dogs pulled her away, another cyclist likely in their crosshairs.

"What do you have there?" Jim asked.

"I landed on this phone," I told him. I looked at the iPhone in my hand, and then turned it over. When I saw the custom phone case, with a photo of a couple I had already seen too much of this weekend, I let out an exasperated sigh. The accident had gone from being a curse to a blessing.

"We have to call Wolsey," I stated through my chattering teeth.

"You look like a drowned rat," Wolsey observed dryly upon arriving to find me sitting on a boulder, wrapped in a towel, dripping water into a newly developed pond at my feet. My shoes were a few feet away, hopefully drying in a sunbeam. But with the humidity as high as it was, that result was yet to be determined.

"I am so sorry!" the dog walker, whose name we had finally learned was Brenda, said for the umpteenth time. She had managed to get control of her charges and returned to the scene of their carnage. They were currently lying in the sun, panting and exhausted from their fun.

I waved a dismissive hand at her, spraying her with water in the process. "Don't worry about it," I grumbled, having had a little while to calm down. "If it hadn't been the dogs, it would have been something else dumping me in the water."

She looked furtively at Jim, who shrugged and nodded. "She's not wrong."

Wolsey refused to be sidetracked. "This," he growled, waving his hand to take in the scene. One of the dogs, a collie, had roused himself and froze in the process of lifting his leg on the dripping seat of my borrowed bike, which was lying on its side beside the path where I had tossed it in anger. As the dog noticed the attention of four humans on him, he dropped his tail between his legs and backed away from the bike. Jim took a moment to go set the bike upright on its kick stand, protecting the seat from any further canine attention.

"Bad dog," Brenda scolded the collie.

Wolsey's lips lifted slightly before he regained his scowl and his train of thought. "This looks familiar."

"Really?" I replied acerbically. "I don't recall ever falling off a bike and into a lake before."

"I would think you would remember that," Marie's voice came from behind Wolsey. I waved half-heartedly at her, not even bothering to ask how she kept arriving when I was at my worse.

"Great, the gang's all here," Wolsey muttered.

I ignored him.

"It was certainly memorable," Jim stated, "even by Casey accident standards."

Marie took in a quick breath, as though she'd just come up with the greatest idea on earth. "That's what we need! A Casey accident scale!"

I groaned but Jim laughed. "With 10 being falling down an embankment and landing on your kidnapper who is planning on shooting you..." he suggested.

"And 1 being stubbing her toe, resulting in it dislocating," Marie added.

"I remember that," Jim chuckled.

"Do you mind?" I snapped. "I am right here."

Wolsey cleared his throat, clearly irritated. Two of the dogs whined in response. "Just tell me what you found in the water this time," he said, determined NOT to be amused.

"Why do you think I found something?"

He glared down at me. "Need I remind you that YOU called ME? And said," he looked down at his small black notebook, "and I quote, 'I found something' unquote."

I had the decency to look sheepish. "There is that," I admitted.

Wolsey was doing a heroic impersonation of a person in possession of a modicum of patience, but the redness creeping into his face belied his effort.

"It's a cell phone," I blurted, reaching out to hand him the piece of evidence.

Brenda gasped. "That's Cindy's phone!"

Wolsey went from irritated to all business. "Are you sure?" He searched his pocket for an evidence bag. A bunch of wrappers that looked suspiciously like they came from Halloween chocolate bars tumbled to the ground. The collie sniffed the fallen wrappers in hopes of a treat, and then retreated in disappointment when he found nothing.

Brenda nodded. "I'd know it anywhere."

"Because of the photo on it," I stated the obvious.

Wolsey held out the evidence bag and I dropped the iPhone into it.

"Won't any prints be washed away?"

He frowned at me. "What, are you a detective now?"

Jim jumped to my defence. "Well, she DID detect a lot in your last case," he reminded the detective.

Wolsey started to formulate a retort but stopped, looking down in shock.

The collie had lifted his leg against the detective's leg. Wolsey nudged the dog away with his foot before it could actually do any damage.

"Control these animals or be fined!" he growled at Brenda, before turning to leave. Two of the dogs growled back at him.

"Do you believe that Cindy is missing now?" Marie called after him.

He froze briefly, but didn't deign to turn around to answer. "Stay out of it!" he yelled back.

THE TRAVELLING KLUTZ

Port Elgin's Pumpkinfest draws tens of thousands of visitors to the town every year. It has grown from a small event celebrating the popular gourd to a massive festival with an event for every taste.

Many of the more than 30 events that are part of Pumpkinfest are a draw in and of themselves. Thousands of people come every year to experience everything from pumpkin carving demonstrations, car and motorcycle shows, celebrity seed spitting competition, and log carving demonstrations.

It makes for a lot of people crowding the town during the two-day event. You never know who you will run into when you are wandering about taking in the sights.

And it is just as likely that, should you actually want to run into someone, they can be very hard to find.

Chapter 8

We hadn't heard anything from Wolsey indicating whether or not Cindy had officially been declared missing. Marie, who often hears these things earlier than everyone else through her various newspaper sources, had also been silent on the matter. That didn't mean we couldn't keep an eye out for her in our wanderings.

"Come on," I told Jim, grabbing my camera and heading to the door of our room.

"But we just got here!" He was as close to whining as I had ever heard him. "Don't you want to enjoy this perfect room for a while?"

I transferred a camera battery from the charger to my camera bag. "I heard that the Queen's Bar and Grill has some seasonal beers on tap," I cajoled. "And we did miss going there during the Pub-Kin Crawl."

His look turned pensive. "I suppose I could be convinced," he said with a wiggle of his eyebrows.

I walked to him and stood on my tip toes to plant a quick kiss on his lips. "We could have dinner..." I tickled his neck with more kisses. "...take in the rest of the car show..." I nibbled his ear lobe. "Check out the motorcycles at the Show and Shine... and then come back..." I planted another quick kiss on his lips. "...for dessert."

I stepped back and met his eyes. He groaned.

"I could go for dessert," he nearly whispered.

I turned away and grabbed my camera bag. "Then we had better get a move on! The sooner we get going, the sooner we will be back."

We enjoyed a lunch of burgers and craft brews at the Queen's Bar and Grill, locally known as QBG. Jim had the Cheeseburger in Paradise: a perfect blend of cheddar, Swiss and mozzarella cheese, with fries. I indulged in the Burger Melt, topped with my favourite combination of bacon, mushrooms, and Swiss cheese, with kettle chips. Afterwards, we headed back to the Cinderella Car Show.

The event was aptly named I thought, as we once again strolled through the classic and antique vehicles lining Goderich Street. I could imagine Cinderella riding about in any of these gilded vehicles as her chariot, only to have it turn into a pumpkin at midnight.

"Keep your ears open," I told Jim as we strolled along the cars on display.

He frowned. "For what?" He was already veering off towards the Corvette Corral. The Saugeen Shores Corvette Club had taken over Mill Street for the event.

"For any news on our missing, jilted, newlywed," Marie answered from behind us, making Jim jump slightly in surprise.

"I wish you would stop doing that!" he grumbled.

"Yeah, it's like you took lessons from Myrna or something," I added.

Marie shrugged. "And I want world peace," she shot back at Jim, ignoring my comment entirely. "Deal with it."

I laughed and linked arms with my friend. "Should we ask to see inside the trunks? Someone could be hidden in one," I suggested.

"Wouldn't hurt," she replied. "You never know what you'll find."

"That's a lot of trunks," Jim pointed out.

"Then we had better get started!" I said in my best chipper voice.

"I know you don't plan on starting any trouble," a distinct voice warned. We all turned with a group sigh to greet Wolsey.

"I really wish people would stop doing that!" Jim snapped.

Marie ignored him. "Why De-tec-tive," she drawled. "What trouble could we possibly start?"

He was about to answer but I beat him to the punch. "We rarely START any trouble," I told him.

"It's usually other people," Marie concurred.

Jim nodded. "It's more like it finds them."

"That's it exactly," I nodded, watching Wolsey's face get redder with each statement.

"Then perhaps you should hide," Wolsey suggested gruffly. "Somewhere far away."

I wagged my camera in the air. "But De-tec-tive," I protested. "I need pictures of the cars and motorcycles for my piece."

Wolsey's eyes swept briefly down the road. I swear that they glazed over.

Men and cars. Sheesh.

"Then might I suggest the '67 Chevy Impala near the end of the street," he said, uncharacteristically helpful.

"Isn't that the car the Winchesters drive?"

He shook his head, puzzled. "What?"

"In Supernatural," Jim provided. "The television show. Casey is a big fan, although I think she watches it for the actors, not the show itself."

"Does it have a large trunk capacity?" Marie asked about the car with an innocent look on her face.

Wolsey was looking back and forth between us at this point, like a person at a tennis match. At the question, his eyes narrowed in suspicion. "Why do you ask?"

I smiled sweetly. "Just curious."

"You are never just curious."

Jim jumped in. "Which trunk would handle the most beer?"

Wolsey turned his suspicious gaze on him. "Are you looking to buy one?" he countered.

"What?" Jim shook his head, his turn to be puzzled. "Of course not. We aren't independently wealthy."

"Then why..."

"You got me!" Marie let out an exaggerated sigh. "I am a vampire who might get caught out in the sun and need a place to hide."

Wolsey looked at the clear sky. "It's sunny now," he observed dryly.

"Which is why we need a big trunk now!" Marie didn't miss a beat. "Quickly, before this SPF 1000 wears off!"

Jim guffawed, earning a glare from the police officer.

"Fine, don't tell me," Wolsey snapped. "Just stay out of trouble.

We decided the plan to see inside of every car trunk was untenable at best. Instead we listened for any sound coming from the trunks as we browsed and took photos. It wasn't long before we crossed paths with Cindy's trio of friends. They were handing out 'MISSING' flyers to whoever would accept them, and jotting down possible sightings of Cindy in a notebook covered in orange glitter.

"Have you seen Cindy?" Helen asked, pressing a flyer into my hand before taking the time to actually look at me. When she did look, she had the presence of mind to look embarrassed. "Oh! It's you!"

I glanced at the flyer, noticing the similarities between it and the 'cheater' poster from earlier. It also featured a photo, this one of a smiling Cindy, with the word MISSING emblazoned across the top instead of BEWARE. Underneath the photo was information on Cindy's age, height, and other details, as well as mention of her medical need of an inhaler. Contact information for her friends concluded the information.

"Have you heard anything?" Velma asked.

Marie shook her head. "And believe me, I've been asking. No one has seen her."

All three young women sighed heavily. "How is that possible?" Lori asked.

"It's a busy weekend," Marie explained. "There is so much to see and do. People aren't looking at other people in the crowd. But we will keep asking and looking. Can we have some of those?"

Helen handed each of us a pile of flyers, thanking us profusely for the help as she did so.

"I have to ask," Jim said. "Are you sure she didn't just go away for a break?"

Lori looked at him as though he were crazy. "She wouldn't go anywhere without her phone!" she exclaimed.

"Or her inhaler!" Velma added. "Not in this heat and humidity."

"In that order?" Jim deadpanned.

I kicked him lightly in the shin. "Seriously?"

Helen narrowed her eyes at my husband. "If she wanted to get away, she would put on the air conditioner and read."

"MY air conditioner!" a male voice exclaimed from behind us.

"Pierre!" Lori yelled. "What have you done with Cindy?"

Cindy's cheating husband, once again dressed impeccably, held up his manicured hands and backed away from the irate young woman. "Me? She's the one who has been attacking me!"

"You slept with her best friend!"

"And apologized," he defended himself.

"Like that makes it all better," I muttered.

Jim slapped me gently on the behind, getting his revenge for earlier.

"She put wanted posters of me all over! All of our troubles are common knowledge now," Pierre continued, ignoring my comment. "Then she dumped all of my things out the window onto the street." He aimed a smug look at me. "Even the dirty laundry."

I guess he heard my comment after all, I thought with a shudder.

"I don't know where she is," he continued, "but I want my air conditioner. She's clearly not using it."

Without warning, Lori launched herself at him, knocking him over. Just as she went in for a swift kick to his privates, a meaty arm snaked around her waist and pulled her off her feet and away from the man on the ground. Her feet continued to flail in the air as if searching for a new target to kick.

"Enough!" Wolsey boomed, drowning out the sound of Marie's camera clicking away as she took photos of the scene. People on the street turned to see what all the fuss was about; turning back to their own business after the detective set Lori down beside him. Jim helped a visibly irate Pierre to his feet.

"Arrest her, Officer!" the Frenchman demanded angrily.

Wolsey kept a grip on Lori's arm to keep her from renewing her attack. He ran his free hand over his brush cut in exasperation. "I have half a mind to arrest the lot of you!" he barked.

For the second time since he'd appeared, Pierre held up his hands in a defensive gesture. "I'm sorry, Detective," he stammered. "I don't want any trouble. I just wanted my air conditioner."

"You want your what?" Wolsey asked incredulously.

"My air conditioner," Peter repeated, not picking up on the fact that Wolsey found his request shocking. "Cindy doesn't seem to be using it, after all."

"Your. Air. Conditioner." Wolsey said slowly. "You don't want your wife."

Pierre rolled his eyes. "Cindy is just being dramatic. We all know she does that. She will show up when all of the attention eases off."

"Why you...!" Lori launched at him again, only to be brought to a screeching halt by Wolsey.

I looked at Pierre in disgust. "How exactly did you convince her to marry you?"

He leveled me with a look so frigid it made my blood turn cold. But just as fast as it appeared, the look was gone. He turned to the detective, his face suddenly the picture of concern.

"Have you heard anything, Detective?"

Wolsey frowned. "No," he growled. "I want all of you to go home and leave this to the authorities."

Pierre nodded. "Yes sir." He turned to go, and then stopped. "About the air conditioner..."

"Nothing leaves that apartment," Wolsey snapped. "Now go, or I WILL arrest each and every one of you."

"What did we do?" I protested.

"I told you to stay out of it."

"We are working," Marie enunciated.

He stared at us through narrowed eyes until we looked away.

"Fine, we're going," I grumbled.

THE TRAVELLING KLUTZ

The municipality of Saugeen Shores, of which Port Elgin is part, has an abundance of trails stretching over 50 kilometres. They are available for hiking and cycling in the spring, summer, and fall, and for snowshoeing and cross-country skiing in the winter. These trails connect MacGregor Point Provincial Park's trails south of town to Port Elgin and north to Southampton.

Take your pick from the gorgeous North Shore Trail, connecting the two towns by running along the Lake Huron Shoreline, or the Saugeen Rail Trail, which also connects the towns by using the former railway route, providing a level and easy path that takes you through rural vistas and residential areas. There are also the Captain Spence Path, which takes you from the base of the Canadian Flag in Southampton to the town's harbour and Pioneer Park; Biener's Bush Trail, in the northwest of Port Elgin and accessible from Concession 10 or Market Street; and Woodland Trail, an easy trail through lush woodlands between the two towns.

A hidden gem of a trail can be found by following the Town Pond Trail at the end of Upper Avenue. The Shipley Trail begins at the end of Mitchell Lane and winds through scenic forests and around spring fed ponds along Lake Huron's post glacial shoreline ridge. You are sure to spot plenty of wildlife here, *but be sure to keep an eye on partially submerged logs for sunning turtles.*

All of these trails are all particularly lovely in the fall with the changing foliage. But remember, just because you are outside, that isn't necessarily a guarantee of actual fresh air.

Chapter 9

We got up the next morning with plans to hike the trails at the north end of town. I was moving pretty slowly thanks to my header off my bike into the lake, but by the time I'd had a hot shower and we descended the stairs to enter the Port in the Storm Cafe, I had loosened up a bit.

"That's quite the bruise you have there," Ilene observed as she brought a carafe of coffee to our table.

"Where?" I asked in alarm, trying to twist to see the back of my arm where she seemed to be looking. Now that I thought of it, my arm was a bit on the sore side.

She chuckled. "On your thigh," she pointed.

"Collecting bruises again I see," Myrna said from behind Jim. He jumped about a foot in his seat, nearly knocking over his coffee cup.

"Will you STOP doing that?"

Myrna chuckled and pulled up a chair. "Sorry, force of habit."

"Seriously," Jim continued. "You're like a ghost sometimes."

"Or a spook," I added, watching the two older women for a reaction. I had developed a far-fetched theory that Myrna, and Ilene by way of association, had been secret agents for the Canadian spy agency CSIS in their younger days.

They both froze for a second and exchanged the oddest look that passed so quickly, I wondered if I had imagined it. Maybe my theory wasn't so far-fetched after all. They both recovered quickly and chuckled, continuing on as if we hadn't said a thing.

Ilene started to pour coffee into the mugs.

"Wait!" Jim exclaimed. "There isn't any *pumpkin* in the coffee, is there?"

She shook her head. "Just good old, high test coffee," she reassured him as she filled his cup. "Just like yesterday. Unless you want a pumpkin latte?"

Jim shook his head a little too desperately, in my opinion.

"But we do have a nice Pumpkin French toast this morning," Ilene offered.

Jim winced, as though the very thought caused him pain. "Pass. Anything else?"

"The old B&B standby," she answered. "Scrambled eggs, bacon and toast."

"Sounds perfect," he said in relief.

"How boring," I teased him. "When else will we get a chance to try pumpkin French toast?"

He shrugged. "You do love French toast, my sweet," he said, reaching over and squeezing my hand. "Go for it."

I smiled at Ilene. "I will have that, with bacon and maple syrup please"

"I will try that too," Myrna said. She turned to Jim. "Coward," she teased.

"Sticks and stones..." he replied.

We heard the door close and turned to see Marie enter. She took a seat next to me.

"Would I be able to get a coffee?" she asked with a sigh.

"I'll bring another carafe," Ilene said and headed for the kitchen.

Marie grabbed a cup from an empty table beside us and poured some coffee from our carafe into it. After taking a big gulp, she sat back with a sigh.

"So, what gives?" I asked.

She took another drink before spilling the beans. "The police have decided that Cindy is indeed missing," she told us, "and they are organizing search parties."

Since we were planning on hiking the trails anyway, we volunteered to join the search in the area of the Woodland Trail. It was just our luck that Wolsey was overseeing the efforts in that particular area.

"Bloody hell," he growled when he saw us. "I cannot get a break."

"I was just thinking the same thing," I retorted.

Wolsey handed Jim a flyer with information on Cindy and the current search area. This one was much more official looking than the one the trio of girls has made up, and had contact information for the police instead.

"You should be glad we turned up, Detective," Jim stated as he looked over the flyer.

"I can't imagine why."

"Why would he be?"

Both the detective and I spoke at the same time. Jim chuckled. "Because, historically speaking, Casey seems to find clues to whatever you are looking for."

"More like trips over them," Wolsey pointed out.

"Or falls into them," Marie added with a laugh.

"Hey!" I protested briefly. I didn't say anything more, because I knew that they had every right to say those things.

Another volunteer walked past us to get a flyer from a volunteer at the entrance of the trail.

"Thank you for your help," we heard Pierre say as he handed the man the flyer.

My surprise at seeing Pierre working as a volunteer in the search was eclipsed as a cloud of scent, one I recognized as Patchouli, wafted over us. The man who had gone past us was wearing an excessive amount, and the wind was blowing it back towards me so fast that I had no time to vacate the area.

I raised my hand to my throat as it started to close in reaction to the offensive scent. With my other hand, I reached out to get Jim's attention.

Typical, I thought. *He doesn't even notice the smell.*

"What?" he asked testily without turning around.

"What's wrong with her?" I heard Wolsey ask in alarm.

I was getting precious little air into my lungs past my rapidly closing airway. I could hear my increasingly pained breaths wheezing loudly in my ears and I stopped reaching for my husband. Instead, I fumbled in my camera bag, in search of my inhaler. I noticed Pierre and the man doused in the cologne turn to see what was happening and backed away quickly in alarm.

Only to step onto a rock and fall with a thud onto my bottom. I landed off of the path into some thick undergrowth, knocking what air I did have in my lungs out of them. My next intake of air sounded like a clogged vacuum cleaner hose.

I felt something being pressed into my hand. I looked down to see my inhaler and relief coursed through me. Another hand guided mine to my mouth and habit took over. I administered two puffs, then sat back in the undergrowth and tried to calm myself while the medication did its work. I turned to smile at my rescuer and Marie smiled back at me.

I searched for Jim and saw him speaking to Pierre and the male volunteer, who looked more than a bit embarrassed, mixed with a tinge on angry. Wolsey was holding back curious people from coming over to where we were and was directing them instead to their portion of the search area.

"I wouldn't want my not being able to breathe to interrupt the De-tec-tive," I gasped.

Marie tsked me. "He knew you were in good hands," she scolded, her defence of the detective surprising me. She handed me a bottle of water and I took a sip.

"You remembered."

"How could I forget? I spent years shooing over-scented people away from my star reporter."

I smiled fondly at the memories her comment elicited. "You took good care of me," I concurred, coughing and taking another drink.

She patted my shoulder. "I still do. Honestly, I don't know how you manage without me with you every day."

"And thank you for that," Jim said as he came and crouched by my side. "How are you doing?"

"Better," I said, and then belied that by having another coughing fit.

"Hmph," Jim groused, rubbing my back. "That was a bad one."

I nodded and used another puff from my inhaler, going far beyond the recommended dosage, but I didn't really care at the moment. "People aren't supposed to bathe in that crap," I complained.

"I told him that, my sweet." Jim looked up as Pierre approached.

"He's gone," Pierre told us. "I had no idea people could react to scents like that."

I reached out and Jim helped me to my feet. "It hasn't happened to me in quite a while, but I'm always prepared." I shook the inhaler in the air before putting it back in my camera bag.

Pierre watched intently as I put it away. "Well, I certainly understand the need," he sympathized. "Cindy has asthma and needs her inhaler. Especially when it's hot and humid like it is now." He paused. "It was lucky that you have that with you."

"I make my own luck," I quipped, then coughed again.

"Really?" Marie asked incredulously.

Jim laughed. "It's usually bad luck though."

I narrowed my eyes at them, and then chuckled, deciding it would be better if they were laughing with me than at me.

Once I was breathing better, we headed out for the shade of the trails. The trees were particularly stunning adorned with the brilliant red and yellow leaves of fall, and I took a few seconds to enjoy the view. While Jim and Pierre, who had decided to stick with us for some reason, kept an eye out for any sign of Cindy, Marie and I took photos of the trail in all of its glory.

"How about you help?" Jim teased.

"I am helping," I replied. "I am documenting the area."

"Uh huh." Jim shook his head and then gave me a quick kiss.

"Cut it out," Marie told us automatically.

"I think it's cute," Pierre said. "How long have you been married?"

"Thirty-five loooong years," Jim joked. He handed me the water bottle just as I was switching my bag to my other shoulder. I set the bag on the ground and accepted the bottle, taking a big drink.

"Are you sure you're ok?" Pierre asked curiously from right beside me. I hadn't seen him move and jumped. "Should you be hiking right now?"

"I'm fine," I said a bit abruptly, causing both Marie and Jim to look at me in shock. I pushed past them and continued down the path in an attempt to prove I was truly fine, leaving them to follow after me.

After a minute or so, I heard Pierre call out. "Oh, Mrs. Robertson! You forgot your bag!"

With a sigh, I stopped and waited for everyone to catch up, stifling a cough as I did.

THE TRAVELLING KLUTZ

Pumpkinfest in Port Elgin is, of course, all about the pumpkins. It is arguably the largest tourist draw of the year to the town. Tens of thousands of people attend the event from all over the province, some coming from as far away as other parts of the country or even the United States.

A large number of growers bring their pumpkins and vegetables to compete at the event. Prizes are awarded to the largest entries down to the 10th place, and junior and novice growers take part in their own event on the Sunday. In 2018, the largest pumpkin weighed in at 1871.5 pounds, while the largest squash weighed 1472 pounds, and the winning watermelon came in at 175 pounds. And that is just the beginning of the variety of large produce you can find and admire at the event.

There's really nothing like seeing a giant vegetable, pumpkin or gourd up close and personal.

Unless it's seeing one of those giant pumpkins facing off against a klutz, and losing. That's even more entertaining.

Chapter 10

After completing our part of the search with nothing else eventful happening, we skipped lunch in favour of seeing what goodies we would find at the Pumpkinfest grounds. When we got back up to the event, there was almost too much variety of food to choose from.

Along with refreshing drinks from Summer Time Lemonade and Just a Cup, and treats such as Prancing Pachyderms Kettle Corn, there was tantalizing food aplenty to tempt every taste. There were meats and cheeses from D-D Meats and Speziale Fine Food. Up for grabs for the main course were foods from Born2Eat's food truck and Best Fajitas in Town, and side dishes from Tornado Potato Canada, Di's Fries, Twisted Tomato and Roasted Street Corn. And for dessert, you could get a twisted cone at Sisters' Twisters, or some of Kiltie's Mini Donuts.

We opted for a small Pumpkin Patch Pizza, curious to taste the special creation, from Grassroots Woodfired Pizza. We also indulged in both a Hawaiian Pineapple and a Triple the Meat pizza, in case the pumpkin one didn't quite hit the spot. Then we got both ice cream cones and mini donuts to finish things off.

After getting more than our fill, we headed for the weigh off area where I could get some photos of the giant produce.

"I wish I could find out what happened to that giant pumpkin," I lamented.

"There are lots of them here," Jim pointed out.

I snapped a photo of a toddler looking up at a massive pumpkin, and then quickly got permission to use the photo and his information from his mother. "But these are real," I finally replied.

"That's the point."

"I wanted to get a picture of the metal one," I clarified.

"If I remember correctly, it was a bit of an eyesore," he recalled dryly.

"Eye of the beholder, my love."

We followed the toddler and his parents to the midway where I took photos of children on rides and plastering their fingers and faces with candy floss.

"Let's go before we see all of that sugar come back up courtesy of that roller coaster," Jim joked.

We turned to leave and nearly collided with Myrna and Andrew.

"Sheesh!" I exclaimed. "Are you two following us?"

"Of course not dear," Myrna answered with a laugh. "We just came up to see what was going on."

"Too bad Ilene couldn't come with you."

Myrna smiled. "Oh, she can't come to Pumpkinfest," she said mysteriously.

"You mean she's too busy at the B&B to get away?"

"Oh, no. She has staff. She can leave," Myrna levelled me with a knowing look. "She isn't a prisoner there, after all. Just the owner."

Andrew had gone to chat with Jim, so I took the opportunity to try to get Myrna to say something, anything really, that wasn't cryptic.

"Then why didn't she come with you?"

Myrna watched a mother try to get a candy apple out of her daughter's hair without resorting to scissors. Clearly distracted, she actually answered my question.

"Well, Ilene was banned when she was around your age," she told me. "In some ways, you remind me of a younger Ilene. Maybe that's why I took to you so well in Kincardine."

I smiled at the compliment, but I wasn't about to get sidetracked. "How do you get banned from Pumpkinfest?" I asked, determined to keep the line of conversation going.

Myrna smiled, clearly revisiting a fond memory. She patted my hand. "You will have to ask Ilene that dear. It isn't my story to tell."

I sighed in exasperation. And I had been doing so well! I tried a different tack. "How did you two become friends?"

A volunteer handed Myrna a flyer with Cindy's photo on it and she paused to glance at it. I was about to give up when she answered. "Ilene and me? We were in the same dance troupe."

I blinked. "You dance?"

She laughed. "Not all of us trip over own feet," she teased. "Or at least we didn't used to." She held up the flyer. "Any news?"

So much for getting more information out of her. Maybe I could press Ilene for answers later. I was having trouble imagining the extremely put-together artist and B&B owner doing anything that would warrant getting banned from Pumpkinfest.

"Nothing," I answered Myrna's question with a shake of my head. "As far as I know, anyway. The search we were part of didn't turn up anything."

She tsked. "I heard you had some excitement during that search today,"

I shrugged. "Just a reaction to heavy cologne. I used my inhaler." I unconsciously reached into my camera bag as I spoke to assure myself that my inhaler was where it was supposed to be. "It's gone!" I exclaimed in a panic.

"What's gone?"

"My inhaler!" I started to search through the bag in case it had been knocked into a different spot, such as the catch all at the bottom. "It's not here!" I cried in alarm.

I felt Jim's hand on my shoulder and calmed a bit. "What did you lose?" he asked.

I looked up at him plaintively. "My inhaler."

He frowned. "It must have fallen out when you dropped your bag earlier. Did you bring an extra?"

I gave him a withering look. "What do you think?"

"Hey!" He said, holding up his hands and backing away a bit. "I'm just checking!"

111

"Sorry," I told him, embarrassed at my poor reaction.

He pulled me into a hug and I tucked my head under his chin. "I understand, my sweet," he comforted me. "Well, we had better go get the spare, before you run into another overly aromatic person."

"We'll go with you," Andrew offered. "We have had enough of crowds for one day."

"Besides," Myrna added, "if you ask Ilene why she got banned, I want to be there to see her answer."

Jim looked inquisitively at me.

"I'll explain on the way back," I told him.

The unseasonable mid afternoon heat and humidity continued to get more and more oppressive and it was a relief to reach The Mariner's Rest. The air conditioning hit us like a blast of arctic air as we entered the building. Almost as one we sighed in relief.

"You're all back," Ilene observed in surprise as she took in the group of us. We were all sweaty and disheveled from the hot walk, while she looked cool and collected, not a hair out of place.

"It was just too hot to stay out any longer," I told her. "This kind of heat is for the young."

She rolled her eyes. "You are young dear," she told me. "Now, these two, on the other hand..." She waved a hand at

Myrna and Andrew. "I believe they were here when the town was founded."

"And here I was, feeling guilty," Myrna retorted. "I certainly don't feel that way any longer."

Ilene narrowed her eyes at her friend. "Who wants lemonade?" she asked after a momentary pause.

"I do!" Marie called out as she came in and joined us. I waved to her as she stopped to stand directly in front of the cool air from the air vent.

"You aren't even going to ask?" Andrew asked Ilene in surprise.

"Don't have to. I'm sure it will come out. It always does." She waved us into the empty dining room. "Go ahead and I'll get the lemonade."

"And cookies?" Jim suggested.

"You are eating too many goodies," I told him as we sat at one of the larger tables.

"What are you implying?"

"I'm not implying, I'm out and out saying it. If you don't lay off the treats you will be less beefcake and more sponge cake."

Andrew guffawed. "She got you!" he laughed, clapping Jim on the shoulder.

Jim released a put upon sigh. "I need the energy to keep chasing after my sweet wife."

"Uh huh," I answered. "You keep telling yourself that."

Ilene returned with a tray holding two pitchers of ice cold lemonade, a stack of glasses covered with various images of pumpkins, and a plate of pumpkin shaped sugar cookies.

"I will be glad when I can put the pumpkin dishes away for another year," she told us as she handed out the glasses and poured generous helpings of lemonade. I noticed that the ice cubes were in the shape of little pumpkins as well.

"The ice cubes are a nice touch," I told her.

"You still have to get through Thanksgiving," Myrna began.

"I have harvest and turkey themed dishes for that."

"...and Halloween."

"Jack o' Lanterns..."

"Which are pumpkins."

"...and ghosts and witches and cats..." Ilene sat down and sipped on her lemonade. "Isn't there something else you would rather be doing than harassing me?" She wiggled her eyebrows at the older couple.

Jim choked on his cookie.

"Nowhere I would rather be right now," Myrna stated smugly.

Ilene frowned, suspecting something was up. She turned to me. "Any news out there on Cindy?"

I shook my head. "Not that I've heard. But in this humidity, if she's asthmatic and needs her inhaler, she could be in real trouble."

Everyone murmured in agreement.

"Speaking of which," Jim said after washing down the last of his cookie, "Casey lost her inhaler. Did anyone turn one in here?"

Ilene shook her head, concerned. "Do you have a spare?"

I nodded my mouth too full of sugar cookie to answer. Myrna caught my eye and nodded conspiratorially at me. I sighed, nearly choking on crumbs in the process.

"So," I said after a few coughs and a sip of lemonade. "How does one go about getting banned from Pumpkinfest, Ilene?"

Ilene closed her eyes for a moment, like a person searching inside for the strength to remain calm. I got the distinct impression this wasn't the first time she had to do so when around her friend. When she opened her eyes, it was to glare at Myrna.

"Really?"

"It just came up," Myrna said, barely containing her laughter.

"You do remember that I know things about you too, don't you, you old bat?"

Myrna stopped laughing. "None of my stories are funny though," she said.

"Ear of the beholder," Ilene shot back.

They stared at each other until I broke the silence.

"So?" I prodded.

"You. Will. Pay." Ilene told Myrna.

For her part, Myrna just shrugged. She didn't seem too concerned.

The two of them were putting me in mind of an older version of two other women I knew very well. I looked over at Marie and her smile told me that she was having the exact same thought.

Ilene sighed. "Fine. When I was young..."

"...er."

"What?"

"Younger. You weren't exactly young."

"And you were never young," Ilene snapped, losing her cool.

"Are you two sure you two are friends?" Marie asked dryly.

Ilene ignored her. "I was about your age," she continued, pointing at me, "which incidentally Myrna thinks is old."

"It's not young."

"Hey!" I protested.

"We went up to Pumpkinfest and were looking at this monster of a pumpkin, at least 1,500 pounds."

"The pumpkin, not Ilene," Myrna deadpanned.

Ilene shook her head. "So I asked Myrna to take my photo with it..."

"There weren't selfies back then."

"And I stood on one of those milk cartons..."

"It was a rickety thing."

"And I lost my balance and fell."

"I told you that you reminded me of her," Myrna told me.

"There are worse people to be compared to," I said, trying to be diplomatic.

"Thank you!" Ilene gushed.

"I'm not sure that was a complement," Jim put in his two cents worth.

We all turned to stare at him.

"Carry on," he laughed with a wave.

"And that's it," Ilene said, starting to stand.

"Oh no you don't!" Myrna exclaimed, pulling Ilene back into her seat.

Ilene sighed. "Fine!" she said. She took a long drink of lemonade. "Had I known there was going to be an inquisition, I'd have included some vodka in this."

We just all stared at her, waiting for her to continue.

"It turned out that the pumpkin in question was rather ... ripe."

"And soft," Myrna added.

"And I fell...into it."

Myrna laughed at the memory. "Literally."

Ilene finally cracked a smile, lighting up her beautiful face and highlighting her laugh lines. "It gave a new meaning to the words smashing pumpkins, that's for sure." Then she giggled like a teenager.

"The thing kind of exploded." Myrna was having no problem sharing the story now, I noticed.

"There was pumpkin everywhere," Ilene chuckled.

"It splattered anyone unfortunate to be in the splash zone," Myrna said between guffaws.

"And I had to clean it out of places I would rather not say," Ilene finally broke down into a full-fledged laugh at the surprised looks on our faces.

"So they banned her from coming back."

"They said I was a menace," she wheezed.

"I've been called that," I commiserated. "Too many times to count."

We all laughed some more, and the lighthearted mood carried on into the afternoon.

One of the really nice things about the trails in the Port Elgin area is that there are trails for all different levels of usage.

For the more adventurous hikers, you can indulge your nature loving instincts on more challenging trails. But for those who have a need to get out of doors but can't quite handle an abundance of rough terrain, hills, and valleys, there is the Saugeen Rail Trail.

Built along the former rail line, the Rail Trail is a surfaced, flat expanse of trail running steadily between Port Elgin and Southampton. Cyclists are found regularly on the trail, as are hikers, joggers, and walkers, who all enjoy the flat, steady trail. It is also an excellent option for those with mobility issues, as it is handicapped accessible.

In fact, the trail allows people of all abilities to enjoy the out of doors as it winds through neighbourhoods, butterfly gardens and rural areas.

Just remember that even the steadiest of trails can still trip you up if you aren't careful.

Chapter 11

At the heavy sound of the front oak door closing, we all looked up to see a harried looking detective.

"De-tec-tive," Marie drawled. "You look like something the cat dragged in."

"And that's saying something," I said under my breath, drawing snickers from both Marie and Jim, and Myrna and Ilene.

It was an indication of his state of mind that Wolsey didn't rise to the bait.

"Any of that lemonade left?" he asked.

Ilene vacated her seat and waved him to take her place. "Sit down and rest," she told him sympathetically. "You look exhausted."

"Even more than usual," I added.

"I'll get more lemonade and cookies from the kitchen," Ilene continued with a warning glance in our direction.

The detective's Eeyore impersonation seemed to be bringing out the mother hen in our hostess.

Wolsey eased into the chair with a groan, but otherwise remained uncharacteristically silent.

"Bad day?" Andrew finally broke the silence.

"Wolsey shook his head."Remind me to stay in my own jurisdiction from now on." His voice was laden with exhaustion and even I started to feel sorry for him.

Until he turned his gaze on me, that is. His eyes narrowed. "I should have made sure you three would be far away before I agreed to fill in here."

Jim put a hand on my arm. "Come on Ed," he protested. "You can't possibly blame us for any of the things that have happened here."

"And yet, here you are, smack dab in the middle of it," he retorted. "Just like the last time."

"I'm just doing my job," Marie snapped. "Although I'm beginning to think it might have been wiser to stick to my own beat too."

"Traitor," I snarled at her, only half in jest, before turning to the detective. "And I'm just doing my job too, by the way."

"Has it occurred to you detective," Myrna opined, "that you are the common thread?"

Wolsey growled deep in his throat, his colour rising. He drew in a breath to, I assume, argue the point, but was interrupted.

"Fresh lemonade," Ilene sang cheerfully as she entered the room. "And since my stash of cookies seems to have been devoured, I brought you some muffins instead." She studied Wolsey. "You looked peaked, detective."

The mention of muffins definitely got his attention, and he showed signs of perking up. "Are they pumpkin?" he asked.

"Of course."

A flash of disappointment crossed his face but disappeared quickly as he practically inhaled one of the muffins. Far be it for Wolsey to turn down baked goods. "Thank you," he mumbled as he reached for a second muffin.

Marie waited until his mouth was full before asking, "So, how goes the investigation?"

Wolsey drew in an exasperated breath and promptly choked on muffin bits. Andrew obligingly walloped him between the shoulder blades until the coughing stopped.

The timing couldn't have been better, in my humble opinion.

After a long drink of lemonade, Wolsey actually answered the question. "There is still no sign of Cindy," he told us. "Her friends insist that she wouldn't up and leave, and they are adamant that her husband is obsessed with her."

"So obsessed that he slept with her best friend?" Jim scoffed.

Wolsey shrugged and had another long drink of lemonade.

"But he has been out with the search parties, handing out flyers and helping every way he could," Jim pointed out. "He seemed genuinely concerned for his wife."

"Yes, he does seem to be worried," Wolsey agreed.

We were all silent for a moment.

"But if she didn't leave, and if Pierre had nothing to do with her disappearance," Marie countered, "What happened to her?"

I picked up her train of thought. "Did she have any enemies?"

Wolsey snagged his third muffin. "Not that we've been able to determine," he mumbled around another mouthful.

For someone who had seemed disappointed on the flavour of the muffins, he certainly had no problems actually eating them.

"Maybe she had an accident," Ilene suggested.

"Can you imagine that?" I joked, but only got a few chuckles for my attempt at lightening the mood with humour.

"Where have you looked so far?" Myrna asked.

"We have looked from downtown, north. That includes the trails and woods between here and Southampton."

"So what's next?" Marie asked, taking notes furiously.

"We head south," Wolsey answered as he drained his glass of lemonade.

"Well, we were heading to the rail trail," I told him. "We can look there."

"Excellent." Wolsey stood, looking slightly better than he had when he arrived. "If anyone else wants to join the search, we will be meeting in the Canadian Tire parking lot."

He started for the door, and then turned to Ilene. "Thanks for the pick me up," he said, pulling out his wallet.

Ilene waved him away. "You are welcome Detective," she said. "Just find that poor girl."

"Man, it's hot!" I complained, mopping sweat from my brow. "I haven't sweat like this in October before."

"I thought that ladies didn't sweat," Jim teased.

"That's an 'alternative fact' that we ladies have encouraged over the years," I explained, making air quotes when I spoke.

We walked south along the rail trail, a wide, even path that took advantage of land previously used by the railroads. The part we were currently on was in the shade provided by trees on the west side, but we could see into residential yards to the east. We had stopped to have a drink of water out of the glare and heat of the sun, but it didn't feel much better in the shade.

"I'm even sweating under my boobs," I continued to complain. I looked up at Jim mischievously. "You know how that is, cookie man," I teased.

He poured some water on his hand and flicked it in my direction in response.

"Nice try. Do it again. It's refreshing."

He shook his head. "Just hurry up and get your pictures so we can go somewhere cool."

I took another drink and closed my water bottle. "I want to get a shot of the bridge up ahead, and then we can head back."

We walked in companionable silence for a while.

"Have you considered that Cindy could have just gone away on her own for a while," Jim asked, breaking the silence.

"Clearly you have."

He shrugged.

"What millennial would go away without her phone?" I asked pointedly.

Jim snickered. "Those are replaceable," he pointed out. "She might have chucked it into the lake in a fit of pique..."

"Listen to you, using new words."

He ignored me. "Pierre could have been hounding her to forgive him or something. That could have made her angry enough to toss it. And if you want to get away from it all, what better way to do so than ditching your phone nowadays?"

"I suppose that has a certain logic to it," I conceded.

"After all, we managed without the darn things when we were that age."

"Were we ever that age?" I sighed. "Sometimes I think things would be better without cell phones, though."

"Preaching to the choir," Jim muttered. "Although, just in this year alone, it's been a good thing we've had them. To call 911 for you."

"Whatever," I laughed. We walked quietly for another few minutes.

"She left her puffer," I added, pulling mine from shorts pocket and waving it in the air.

"You LOST one."

"What's your point?"

Jim rolled his eyes. "How many spares do you have?"

"Hmm, let me think. One in my purse, one in the car...my bike bag...my gym bag...I think that's it."

"Your camera bag?"

"No, I usually just move the one from my purse into there, because I never carry both."

"MY point," he stressed, "is that if you leave one behind or lose one, odds are that you are still well stocked."

I sighed in concession. "You're right."

"What was that?" He put a hand behind his ear. "I'm not sure I heard that correctly."

I laughed. "You are right," I repeated. "She probably had backups of backups. And she may have just gone away."

Jim's attention was focussed on the bridge ahead and he was suddenly ignoring me. Which was odd, since he didn't get to hear me say he was right that often. Even when he was.

"What is it?" I asked in alarm.

He pointed at a light jacket draped over the railing of the bridge we were approaching. "Does that look familiar to you?"

I stared at the piece of clothing for a moment before I placed where I had seen it before. "It looks like the jacket Cindy is wearing in her missing picture!"

A breeze picked up at that moment and the jacket began to lift off of the railing. I rushed forward to grab it before it blew away.

Rushing, by the way, is something that a klutz should never, ever do.

I reached the end of the structure and stubbed the toes of one foot at the transition between the walkway and the platform. Before I could register my predicament, I was falling forwards onto the bridge. I reached for the railing on the way down and was rewarded by a ripping sound.

Then my knees cracked down on the wooden bridge deck, followed briefly by my hands, forearms and elbows, before I belatedly rolled onto my back. My head snapped back and hit the boards with a clunk.

Jim was already beside me, looking down in concern.

"Are you okay?"

I held up Cindy's torn jacket. "At least I got the jacket."

Then I gingerly lay back with a groan.

THE TRAVELLING KLUTZ

There is nothing like a petting zoo to bring out the kids - and bring out the kid in all of the adults. Perhaps that's why the Pumpkinfest organizers decided to add a petting zoo to the weekend festivities.

The Little Tracks Petting Zoo, located at the corner of Mill and Bricker Streets, sits conveniently next door to the midway, presumably so that families can have fun at multiple venues without having to go too far. The petting zoo, billed as an event that 'brings the farm to you', allows the young, and the young at heart, to get up close and personal with all sorts of animals. You will find up to 30 different types of farm animals, from perennial favourites to more exotic breeds. There is everything from donkeys, goats, cows and chickens to the very popular alpacas.

Of course, one must remember that, when getting up close and personal with the animal kingdom, the unexpected can and often will happen. Those animals are quite friendly, right up until the moment they aren't.

Chapter 12

"Tell me again how it got torn to shreds?" Marie was staring at me, her hands on her hips and a look of disbelief on her face. She had caught up with us shortly after I had gone on my little trip.

I frowned at her. "Don't look at me in that tone of voice."

She rolled her eyes at me.

"And it's hardly in shreds," I continued. "It's just a tear." I held up the jacket in question. "I admit, it's a long tear..."

She contained her smile, but just barely.

"Let me guess. You went to retrieve the jacket and ... um, tripped?"

"It was going to blow away."

"Of course it was. So you..."

"Ran to capture crucial evidence..."

"And tripped," Jim confirmed acerbically.

She turned to look at him. "So on the CAS scale, what did this rate?"

He looked confused. "The what scale?"

"The CAS scale. The Casey Accident Scale," she spelled out for him. "Don't tell me that you've forgotten already."

Jim laughed. "No, I haven't forgotten. I just didn't realize that we were using an acronym."

"Well we are. So, how did it rate?"

Jim thought for a moment. "Well, she DID hit her head, so I'd have to go with a four."

Marie nodded and turned back to me. For my part, I was doing my best to not look amused by their new pick-on-Casey game. "That still doesn't explain how the jacket got torn," she pressed. "Unless it was already?"

I shook my head and her hopeful expression fell. "That would make for a better story for you, I admit. But no, it was fine. It caught on that nail." I nodded my head at the side of the bridge, instantly regretting the movement as pain stabbed behind my eyes.

"Which would have been fine, if she hadn't been depending on it to save her from falling," Jim added.

I turned on him, wincing at the effort. "You. Aren't. Helping."

He smirked and I threw the jacket at him.

Only to have it intercepted by a meaty hand.

"Tell me you are not playing capture the lag with a piece of evidence," Detective Wolsey growled.

Marie snorted and I looked over the railing I was leaning on to determine if leaping over it to escape Wolsey's wrath was an option.

It wasn't. As though I was capable of such a feat of athleticism anyway. Instead, I faced him head on.

"Oops?"

Wolsey turned red and ran a hand over his bristly hair. Then he held a hand out to Jim. "I'll take that before you two do any more damage to it," he said.

Jim handed the garment over and filled Wolsey in on its discovery, while Marie and I dissolved into giggles. After a few moments, Wolsey cleared his throat to get our attention.

"Anything you would like to add?"

I looked at my husband. "Anything I would like to add?" I repeated.

Jim shook his head. "No, my sweet. I'm pretty sure that I covered it all."

I smiled sweetly up at Wolsey. "Nope."

He sighed and dropped the jacket into an evidence bag. "Good. Now, if you could go back the way you came, we will process the scene."

"We're out of here!" Jim grabbed my arm and started to pull me away.

I planted my feet firmly and stood my ground. "But my pictures," I protested.

"You took a ton of this spot the last time we were here," he pointed out.

"That was last summer."

"I don't think it's changed much in that time," Marie told me as she walked by on her way to ask the detective some questions.

"Besides," Jim added, "I'm sure you will have more than enough pictures from this trip to use."

"I like having choices," I grumbled.

"Why are you still here?" Wolsey snapped.

We bid a hasty retreat.

Once we got back downtown, my sore muscles had loosened up and the headache I'd developed after hitting my head on the bridge deck had subsided. I felt well enough to go take some pictures at the Little Tracks Petting Zoo. Photos of animals were always guaranteed to tug at the readers' heartstrings.

Truth be told, I wasn't ready to try sitting down anywhere on my sore behind.

"I want to pet the alpacas," I said excitedly.

"You mean get pictures of them?"

I grinned at Jim. "Of course. That's exactly what I meant."

The petting zoo was sandwiched between the midway, with its abundance of rides and screaming children, and the

Kiddie Karnival, which featured plenty of games and prizes for the kids. I thought it unfair that the animals not only had to put up with being mauled by strangers, but with the noisiest events of the festival taking place around them as well.

That didn't stop me from embracing my inner child and heading for the critters, however. I only stopped to take some photos, and to buy a handful of carrot bits for the alpacas from a farmer at a strategically located table. I bypassed the typical farm animals - donkeys, cows, pigs, goats and chickens - and zeroed in on the alpaca enclosure.

There were three alpacas penned together in the enclosure. One was large, standing almost eye to eye with me. The animal's coat was the cozy brown that brought to mind a warm coffee with milk on a cold winter's morning.

The second alpaca was slightly smaller, with a darker brown coat that was almost black. It had a fluffy tail that it seemed unable or unwilling to keep still. The third alpaca was smaller, almost pure white, and much more excited to be there than its pen mates were. Once it caught sight of a hand bearing carrots, the smaller alpaca would make a beeline for the treat, with no regard as to what or who might get in its way. More than once it ran into one or both of the other animals which, much to the delight of onlookers did not take kindly to the jostling. Their reactions ranged from pushing back to spitting to kicking at the smaller alpaca. For its part, the white alpaca would just continue on its way with an irrepressibly enthusiastic bound.

I decided that the white one had to be pre-teenaged, whatever that would be in alpaca years.

I reached the edge of the enclosure closest to the dark coloured alpaca and held out my hand palm up, offering it some carrot. The placid creature looked at me with what I swear was disdain before actually sighing and approaching my hand daintily. Its velvety lips brushed my palm as it took the treat and I reached out to pet the velvety fur on its head.

I was thrilled with the moment, for the short time it lasted.

The young alpaca clued in that someone else was getting fed the food it wanted all to itself. It moved so fast I barely had time to wonder if it was a were-alpaca. Then it plowed into the darker creature, hitting my arm in the process. The alpaca eating from my hand barely budged.

I wish I could say the same for me.

The force of an adolescent quadruped ramming my arm combined with my natural instinct to jump back in an attempt at protecting myself, with predictable results.

I jumped backwards, crashing my arm on the enclosure on my way, knocking a section of the pen over. At the same time, my feet hit a wet patch of ground where someone had spilled something both liquid and sticky, and I fell backwards.

There was no time to attempt to roll, even had I thought of it. I fell hard on my already sore rear end, momentum pushing me sliding back through the sticky liquid on the ground.

At least I didn't hit my head, I thought, just before I noticed the falling piece of fencing. I tried to scramble backwards, but couldn't get any traction. The piece of enclosure slammed down on my shins and I screamed out in shock and pain.

Which, of course, frightened the trouble-making, adolescent alpaca. Because, of course it would.

Jim had just started to come to my rescue when the flighty creature realized it was no longer penned in. Like any reasonable being, it seized upon the unexpected freedom, leapt over the fence piece, and flew past us.

Which I really would not have cared about, had it not stomped on my hand, which was still resting on the ground, on its way past.

The other two alpacas stood by regally and surveyed the damage.

"Are you okay? Jim moved the fencing off of my legs, putting it aside on the ground. He then looked like he didn't know where it was safe to touch me.

My forearm throbbed from where it had hit the fence and my shins were burning with pain. I followed his glance down to my throbbing hand. There was actually a red spot developing in the shape of an alpaca's two toed foot. To make it worse, there was a cut along one side, where my hand had been rammed into the placidly feeding alpaca's teeth.

Its lips may have been velvety, but its teeth definitely had not been.

But what really drew a gasp from me was the sight of my hand resting in, not spilled pop like I had assumed, but disgustingly liquid vomit. Vomit that was mixing with red as my hand bled into the mixture of what looked like pop, candy floss, hot dogs, and dropped carrot bits.

It was all I could do to keep my own stomach contents down. Especially when I remembered that I had slid through the mess on my behind.

"Help me up?" I plaintively asked my husband.

He hesitated. Not that I could really blame him

Who am I kidding? Of course I could blame him. And I would. For a long time.

I glared at him and he sighed. Marie, who had appeared towards the very end of the debacle, handed him a few napkins from her Tardis of a camera bag, and he reached down to take my uninjured yet vomit covered hand in his napkin-protected own.

"Oww, Ow, Ow," I whined as my shins protested.

"What's that?" Marie pointed to a spot on the ground where the fencing had collapsed. The sight of something sparkling in the sun distracted me from my injuries.

"It looks like a bracelet," I observed distractedly.

"That's Cindy's!" a now familiar man's heavily accented voice exclaimed. We turned to see Pierre.

"Ah, great," I muttered. I looked up at Jim. "I just wanted to pet an alpaca, honest."

THE TRAVELLING KLUTZ

You are never at a loss for dining options when you are in Port Elgin. On the contrary, there may be too many choices, depending on the length of your stay. You just may not have enough time to get to every excellent culinary experience.

There literally is something for everyone. There are a number of casual dining choices, from national chains to mom and pop style restaurants, with meals ranging from pub grub to light lunches. Some excellent examples of these are the chain franchises of Boston Pizza and Pizza delight, and local restaurants such as The Woodpecker Fresh Dining & Lounge, Aunt Mabel's Country Kitchen, Allan's Fireside Grill, and the Wismer House.

For more formal dining, you have a wide choice of international cuisine. You can indulge in excellent Italian food at Ristorante Rosina, get a taste of Swiss food at Andre's Swiss Country Dining, get your fill of Chinese food at Lido Gardens, or enjoy a traditional British fish dinner at Lord Elgin Fish and Chips.

And of course, fast food is abundant for a quick bite, with Canadian chains Harvey's, Swiss Chalet, and Tim Horton's leading the list that includes mainstays such as McDonald's and Subway.

Whatever your desire, you will find something to satisfy your tastes in Port Elgin. It's a place where the people are friendly and they treat you like family.

Of course, if you remember the last holiday get together with family, being treated as such could be either good or bad.

Chapter 13

Detective Wolsey was grouchily surveying the damage while Marie busily photographed it all. I was careful to keep my head turned whenever I saw her camera pointed in my direction.

"I cannot wait to hear how you caused all of this," Marie said gleefully.

"I can," Wolsey barked.

"I didn't cause it at all!" I protested. "That innocent looking, four-legged spawn of Satan is to blame."

The alpaca in question, which had only gone so far as the table that featured the carrot bits for sale, turned to look innocently at us, as though saying, "Who, me?"

"Don't let him fool you with that pure white fur and cute face," I grumbled. "He's a trouble maker."

"Sounds like someone I know," Wolsey grumbled.

A paramedic finished cleaning and bandaging the cut on my hand and I smiled my thanks at her.

Marie whispered something to Jim. "What now?" I snapped.

"She said this one looks like a score of seven on the CAS scale," Jim informed me.

I rolled my eyes, but the comment had caught Wolsey's attention. "What scale is that?" he asked.

While Jim and Marie explained their new amusement to the detective, I ignored them and used a handful of nearby hay to try to wipe my clothes clean. Once Wolsey had stopped chuckling, I spoke up, changing the subject.

"Your silly scale aside," I groused, "the real issue is that bracelet." I lowered myself onto a bench, not sure at this point what hurt the most or what part of myself I should be favouring.

Wolsey had the bracelet in yet another evidence bag. I hadn't been able to get a good look at it, but had noticed that it was a gold infinity symbol on a fine gold chain.

"I gave that to her last Christmas," Pierre said wistfully. He turned to Wolsey, a look of hope on his face. "Does that mean she was here?"

Wolsey handed the evidence bag to the same young uniformed officer we had seen at the hot dog incident before answering. "It's starting to look like she might still be in the area. We are not ruling out anything just yet."

"But if she's here, why is she avoiding us?" Pierre whined.

"Really?" Marie interrupted, her tone communicating her surprise that the man could be so utterly clueless. "You can't think of one reason why she wouldn't want to see you?"

Wolsey frowned at her before answering Pierre. "Well, that's the million dollar question, isn't it?" he told the visibly distraught man.

We all were silent for a moment.

"You stink," Marie informed me.

"Gee thanks."

"What are friends for?"

Wolsey snickered. "Why don't you go get cleaned up?" he suggested. "If I need you, I'll send you a text."

I sighed. "Good idea."

I reached out for help and Jim pulled me to my feet. I leaned heavily on him as I started to limp away.

"Wait!" Wolsey barked, and then turned to speak to the officer to whom he'd given the evidence bag. The officer nodded and Wolsey turned back to us.

"This officer is going your way and you don't look up to the walk," he told me. "So you get to ride in the cruiser."

Out of habit I opened my mouth to argue, but I thought better of it when Jim's nudge to stop me from declining the offer hit my throbbing hand.

"Wonderful," I said, only halfway sarcastic.

By the time I'd had a long, soothing shower and felt somewhat human again, Jim had arranged for us to head back downtown for dinner at the well known Lord Elgin Fish and Chips restaurant. The establishment had been voted the number two fish and chip restaurant in the entire country by Canadian Living Magazine. It was a must visit every time we were in Port Elgin.

We took a cab to the restaurant, where Jim had reserved a table for the group. Marie, Myrna and Andrew were already there, but Ilene had bowed out, citing work at the Bed & Breakfast that she had to look after.

Jim had texted Marie our drink order and the two pints of local craft beer arrived at the table at almost the exact same time as we did. I eased slowly into my chair and took a long drink, followed by an equally long sigh.

"You are getting too old for this," Marie teased.

"Tell me about it," I groaned.

"Oh please!" Myrna laughed. "Talk to me in 20 years."

"You have to be the luckiest person I know," Andrew observed out of the blue.

I choked on some of the drink I had just taken. "What? I don't consider any of these bruises or pulled muscles to be evidence of my outstanding luck."

"Anyone else would be in the hospital by now," Andrew pointed out. "You must be made of rubber or something."

"Or something," I grumbled.

"You're something else, that's for sure." Wolsey loomed behind me and his sudden input made me jump. "Is there a seat at this table for me?"

"By all means," Jim said. "We were just about to order."

As if on cue, the waiter returned and we did just that. I ordered my favourite haddock and chips, with gravy for the fries, while Jim asked for a cod dinner. Marie, Myrna and Andrew all went with the shrimp dinner while Wolsey ordered a Guinness and the shrimp and fish platter.

Once the waiter left, Marie turned to the detective. "So," she said, "How goes the investigation?"

Wolsey was silent as his drink arrived and took the time to take a sip before answering. "It is looking more and more like Cindy just doesn't want to be found."

"Do you really believe that?" I asked in surprise.

He frowned at me. "Sometimes, people just want to be left alone," he droned with a sigh, sounding like he had already said this repeatedly and not just to us. "She is an adult, and if she doesn't want people to know where she is, that is ultimately her business."

"Can I quote you on that?" Marie pressed.

"No."

"That explanation won't sit well with her friends," Myrna pointed out.

Wolsey sighed and ran his hand over his short cropped head. "No, it definitely did not."

"But if they are so sure she wouldn't just go off..." I began.

"Look!" he barked impatiently. "We have searched. Extensively. And what did we find? Her jacket..."

"Torn up," Jim muttered, getting kicked under the table for his effort.

"...her cell phone..."

"Which no young person would ever behind," Marie interjected.

"Unless they want to be left alone," Myrna argued.

"...and her bracelet," Wolsey continued, ignoring the interruptions. "Which had a broken clasp. All of these things were found in the area, after she was seen last, indicating that she is still in the area."

The food arrived and the conversation paused until the waiter was finished giving each of us our food and taking more drink orders. After the first appreciative tastes, I decided to go on the offensive.

"Her friends say she would never go away without telling someone," I began. "And her apartment was trashed."

"She just had a very public and embarrassing break up," Wolsey countered before putting a large piece of fish into his mouth. "And it looks like she trashed her own place getting rid of her husband's stuff."

"Her husband wants to reconcile," I argued, "so all is not lost."

"He cheated on her!" Marie protested. "With her best friend. She's beyond angry."

I ignored that. "She left without her medication during a heat wave that would require her to have it on hand," I pressed.

"You have spares," Jim countered. "Why wouldn't she?"

147

I shot him a quelling look. "Finding her personal items just seemed...I don't know, convenient," I concluded.

"So, you don't think that she is just hiding out," Andrew broke his silence. "Assuming for the moment that you are right, what do you think could have happened to her?"

I shrugged and turned to my food, stabbing my haddock with my fork and breaking off a crispy piece.

"Well, maybe she had an accident," I suggested before popping the fish into my mouth and sighing with pleasure.

"We did find the jacket at that pretty high bridge," Jim offered, leaving everyone to draw the obvious conclusion that she may have fallen off of the structure. I reached over a squeezed his leg, happy to have him back on my side where he belonged.

Wolsey took another drink before answering. "We checked around and under that bridge. There was no sign of anyone falling off and getting hurt."

"Well, except for Casey," Marie muttered.

"Really?" I snapped at her.

She shrugged. "I gotta tell it like it is," she said as she popped a shrimp in her mouth.

"And I found her phone in the lake. She might have had an accident in the water, dropped it and been washed away," I speculated.

"You 'found' the phone very close to shore," Wolsey countered. "Had she run into trouble so close to shore, she'd have been found. Or helped for that matter."

148

"And it isn't like the lake has much of a current so close to shore," Andrew added.

We were quiet again, eating and thinking of the different possibilities.

"Does anyone else find that Pierre odd?" Myrna asked suddenly. We all looked at her in surprise.

"Odd how?" Wolsey asked.

She shrugged. "I don't know exactly. I can't put my finger on it, but I find him ... creepy?"

"Like a guy that sleeps with his new wife's best friend?" Marie asked sarcastically.

"Maybe that's it," Myrna conceded, but she didn't sound convinced.

"Besides," Jim added. "He has been front and centre in the searches for her. He seems to be really concerned."

"Have you looked into any enemies Cindy might have?" Andrew asked Wolsey.

"From what we can tell, she has none," he answered before stuffing about three shrimp into his mouth. He chewed and swallowed before adding, "She seems to be a popular and well liked person."

Marie pushed back her empty plate. "Well, this is getting us nowhere," she said. "What's the next move, Detective?"

Wolsey drained the last of his beer. "Unless we get some concrete indication to the contrary, we are proceeding on the assumption that she just does not want to be found," he answered. "There is just no indication of any accident or foul play."

I sighed. "That just doesn't feel right."

"We can't go by feelings." Wolsey seemed to wish that he could. "So unless something else comes to light, our hands are tied."

One look around the table told me that I wasn't the only one unhappy with that conclusion.

THE TRAVELLING KLUTZ

This past summer I wrote that residents of the town of Kincardine are adamant about the fact that they have the most beautiful sunsets in Ontario. Drive 30 minutes north of Kincardine, however, and the residents of the town of Port Elgin will tell you that their neighbours are sorely mistaken. Every resident in Port Elgin will tell you that it is their sunsets that are the most breathtaking anywhere.

The town's Wikipedia page even makes mention of the nightly spectacle, saying the town is 'renowned' for its sunsets. In 2007, the entire municipality of Saugeen Shores' sunsets ranked as one of the finalists in the CBC Television Seven Wonders of Canada competition, although they did not make it into the top seven. And Cottage Life magazine recognizes the beauty of the Port Elgin sunsets in its article 10 Spectacular Places to Watch a Sunset in Ontario.

That same article concedes that anywhere along the Lake Huron shoreline makes for wonderful sunset viewing. But that doesn't stop the residents of almost every town along the shore from claiming that their sunsets are the best. One thing is for sure, no one can argue that the bright oranges, reds and yellows, reflecting on the crystal clear, blue water of the lake, aren't a sight to behold.

And while you are admiring the brilliance of nature's canvass, perhaps it will shed some light on other things that need clearing up.

Quiet time has a way of doing that.

Chapter 14

The two of us sat in wicker arm chairs that faced the windows of our upper turret room, availing ourselves of a spectacular view of the sunset over Lake Huron. Currently the sun was a massive orange ball that seemed to be sinking into the water, while its beams of light were reflecting off of some wispy clouds in the sky above to give the entire scene an ethereal quality. The beach area was crowded with people of all ages enjoying both the unseasonably warm weather and the sunset. Sailboats that were usually out of the water by this point of the year, bobbed in the water off shore, and from our viewpoint we could see people on the decks of the closest boats, turned towards the sunset.

I thought that aboard a boat would be the only better place to watch the sunset than the one we were lucky enough to have in the turret of The Mariner's Rest. "I never get tired of watching this," I said with a happy sigh.

Jim nodded and sipped some dry white wine from a pumpkin covered wine glass that was no doubt one of the event themed tableware that Ilene had mentioned looking forward to putting away for another year. The drink elicited a sigh of his own from my husband.

"I know why I sighed," I told him, "But I don't think you were doing it over the sunset."

He chuckled. "It IS a nice sunset."

"But..."

"But I was more into the lack of pumpkin flavour in this wine."

I laughed and felt tension I hadn't been aware of, leave my shoulders. "If you are missing pumpkin, you have only to look at your glass."

"I'm trying not to."

We sat quietly, enjoying the sunset, the pumpkin-free beverage and the air conditioned room. When we had last been outside the humidity had only started to abate for the day. We'd opted for sunset viewing from our room, rather that sweating down on the beach as the sun set. Once inside the air conditioned room, we had brought the glasses and wine to the chairs, put some ice and the wine bottle in a big steel bucket, and settled in, still in our summer clothes, for a relaxing evening. It had been an excellent decision.

We couldn't have enjoyed wine down on the beach. The last thing we needed was to be nabbed by the police for having open alcohol in a public place.

Jim broke the silence. "Do you really think Cindy doesn't want to be found?"

I hesitated. I was loathe to disrupt our moment of silent contentment. "I suppose it's possible," I finally answered.

"But..." Jim could always tell when I had more to say.

"I just can't shake the feeling that something has happened to her."

Jim pondered that, frowning slightly. "Like an accident? Maybe you are just projecting your experiences onto her."

I looked at his dancing eyes and smile, and chuckled. "Maybe," I conceded, "but I think someone took her. Or worse."

The statement hung in the air between us. Jim drained his pumpkin wine glass and pulled the wine bottle from the bucket, dripping ice water on the floor as he did so. He refilled our glasses and returned the bottle to the bucket before sitting down beside me. We clinked our glasses together and then were both silent as the bright ball that was the sun finished its apparent drop into the water.

"But who would want to kidnap her?" he asked once the twilight settled.

"My first guess would be her husband. It's almost always the spouse on television."

"She would be yelling at him constantly..." Jim joked.

"And rightly so..."

"...and he would never get a moment's peace if he did that." He laughed at his own observation. "Besides," he added, "he has been so active in the search. How could he keep an eye on a prisoner and search for her at the same time?"

I conceded the last point with a nod. "Her friends might have spirited her away."

Jim frowned at the suggestion. "Why would you say that?"

"Maybe to keep her from relenting and going back to him. To protect her from getting hurt again."

"Ah, I see where you're going. Keep her away until they're sure that she has come to her senses."

I nodded. "Something like that."

"I don't see it," Jim decided.

I rolled my eyes. "Of course you don't."

"They have been almost over the top with their worry for her."

"It could be an act."

"I just don't get that vibe from them," I said, sipping my wine. "One person could maybe pull off an act like that, but all three?"

We both sat silently for a bit, considering the situation. I realized we would have to turn on a light soon. It might have felt like August outside, but it was still October and the nights came earlier.

"What if a stranger took her?" Jim suggested.

"Why would a stranger take her?"

"Well, she is an attractive young woman. Add to that, she wasn't very low key about being a jilted wife. Maybe someone saw the posters and clothing tossing and marital spat. Maybe the onlooker thought that she was feisty enough to want him for himself."

"Or that she was a damsel in distress who needed protection..."

"Or that she was so badly behaved for a young lady that she merits punishment."

I blanched. "Damn, I hope not."

I drained the rest of my wine from the glass and reached into the bucket to get the bottle. I refilled our glasses and held the bottle up in the air. "Another dead soldier," I lamented, turning it upside down and dropping back into the ice water.

Jim was still considering the latest theory. "If someone with no connection to her took her, she may never turn up," he stated.

I frowned. "Again, I hope that's not it." I sat and considered the situation again. "But maybe we're coming at this from the wrong direction."

"Meaning?"

"Instead of trying to figure out who would take her, how about figuring out WHERE someone would take her?"

"Or where she would hide," Jim added. "But it feels like they have looked everywhere."

"Have they though? Where have they looked again?"

"Wolsey said they called all of the hotels, motels, B&B's and campgrounds."

"And the trails were scoured," I added, unable to hide my wince at the memory of my mishaps.

"Still sore, my sweet?" Jim asked, reaching over and rubbing my upper back.

I sighed as his magic hands eased my sore muscles. "Perpetually, it seems."

He snorted. "I am not even going to consider commenting on that," he said. Instead, he leaned in and kissed me softly. "Perhaps I can kiss you better," he whispered.

A scene from Raiders of the Lost Ark ran through my head. In it, Karen Allen's character of Marion was trying to get romantic with Harrison Ford's character of Indiana, after his actively bad day of fights and falls. He pointed out each and every spot that hurt, and she responded by kissing each of them.

"Perhaps you can at that," I murmured. I pointed to the back of my head. "It hurts here," I whispered.

He rose and obligingly kissed the spot.

I held up my trampled hand. "And here."

Jim gently took my hand and kissed it. I winced a bit, but smiled at him to let him know that I was okay.

I pointed at my sore neck. "And here."

With a smile he nuzzled the spot before kissing it. With his lips still against my neck, he whispered, "Perhaps we should move this to the bed where I can kiss your ouchies better a little more thoroughly."

"Just a little?" I whispered, before nodding in agreement. I allowed him to pull me to my feet.

All thoughts of a certain disappearance were suddenly chased away.

THE TRAVELLING KLUTZ

As in every place on the surface of the planet, Port Elgin has a plethora of out of the way spots that just don't make it onto the typical travel brochures.

For instance, many people find it historically interesting and informative to explore cemeteries, especially those that date back to the founding of the town. At these, you can discover when outbreaks of disease or sudden natural disasters or accidents took town residents before their time. You will also find the tombstones of soldiers who did not come home from war alive, but are remembered nonetheless.

Aside from the historical significance of these sites, cemeteries also provide a peaceful, shady place in which to stroll, respectfully of course, and escape the hubbub of busy, crowded streets. As well, many of the tombstones are works of art and are worth a visit just to see the craftsmanship of the trades people who surviving family members commissioned to honour their loved ones.

There are quite a few cemeteries in the Saugeen Shores area that are worth a visit if you want a day away from it all. The municipality owns and manages the Burgoyne Cemetery on Bruce Road 3, the Pioneer Cemetery on the aptly named Cemetery Road, the Southampton Cemetery on Carlisle Street, and St. Patrick's Cemetery also on Cemetery Road.

Of course, like most municipalities, Port Elgin has cemeteries that were never maintained by the town itself and are therefore not be found in any database. Often, those are the ones with the most interesting information just waiting to be discovered on their graves.

But quite likely the loveliest of the cemeteries in Port Elgin is the Sanctuary Park Cemetery on Eastwood Drive. It is a particularly peaceful, lush, and well cared for cemetery in a less travelled corner of town, perfect for a quiet stroll. The entrance features tall brick memorial pillars that support intricate black cast iron gates. Manicured bushes and trees line the roadways, providing shade the various tombstones and crypts. Here casualties from both World Wars are laid to rest, and visitors are encouraged to pay their respects.

The cemetery is bordered on one side by Elgin Street, and the Mill Creek runs to the east of the property. Directly across the street is a wooded area known as The Pinery, and the area also sits in the shadow of a water tower that services the area. With these surroundings, Sanctuary Park Cemetery is also known for its spooky nature once the sun goes down. As a result, evening strolls in the month of October could provide for an even spookier experience.

Whenever you go for a visit, while you are out walking among the tombstones, be sure to pay attention to what other undiscovered areas are nearby. You never know what you might find.

Chapter 15

We sat alone in the Port in a Storm Cafe, drinking Pumpkin lattes and eating pumpkin muffins, much to Jim's chagrin. I had to promise him that I would never serve him anything pumpkin related once we returned home.

Ilene entered the cafe carrying a stainless steel beverage carafe. She looked as collected as ever and I was certain that nothing much could ruffle her feathers. Over her clothing she wore a white apron bearing an image of both a pumpkin and a takeout coffee cup, above which were the words "Happy Pumpkin Spice Season". Each word was coloured a slightly different shade of orange.

"Nice apron," I observed.

"Thanks," she said. "Starting tomorrow, I switch to a black one that says "Keep calm and gobble, gobble, under a sketch of a turkey."

I laughed. "Never a dull moment, eh?"

She watched Jim finish his latte and push the cup away. "Refill?" she asked innocently.

Jim groaned. "I'll pass, thanks."

"That's a shame," she replied, starting to turn away. "All I have right now is black coffee."

Jim reached out a hand to stop her. "Sold!"

Ilene and I both laughed and watched him take a drink of his coffee like a man getting his first drink of water after crossing the desert.

"So, you will be heading home tomorrow?" she asked me.

"Yes," I told her. "I almost have all of the information and photos that I need."

"What more are you looking for?"

"I wanted to see if I could find something that would work in Halloween, since it's around the corner," I explained. "Maybe something spooky."

"Oh, well then," Ilene said as she sat down beside me, "you will want to head out to Sanctuary Park Cemetery. It's a lovely spot, but it can also be kind of spooky when it's gloomy."

I looked out the window. "It is looking pretty overcast," I observed. "There must be a front coming in."

Ilene nodded. "Hopefully it will break this heat when it does. This has been the hottest Pumpkinfest I can remember."

"I don't doubt it," I said, before turning to Jim. "Well, my darling, if you've had enough coffee, what do you say to heading out to look at the cemetery?" I said the last word in the spookiest voice I could muster.

Jim laughed. "You sound like a vampire with laryngitis."

Ilene laughed as well. "While you're out there, check out The Pinery. It's a woodlot right across the road. You might get some spooky pictures there too."

"Thank you Ilene, we will!"

We drove over to the Sanctuary Park Cemetery, having decided that it was far too hot and humid to bike away from the lake and its cooling breezes. We were both dressed again in shorts and t-shirts, and we both carried a water bottle with us. As soon as we were past the downtown area, the crowds dropped away and it was almost like being in a different town entirely.

We both breathed a sigh of relief as we exited the car.

"Listen to that," I told Jim.

He paused and did as he was told. With a puzzled look on his face, he asked, "Listen to what?"

"Exactly!" I gave him a quick hug before deciding that it was too hot for cuddling and stepped away. "Can you imagine living here and experiencing these crowds every year?" I asked Jim as we joined hands and headed for the cemetery gate.

"Kincardine did get pretty busy during its festivals," Jim pointed out.

"I don't think it ever got quite this busy," I argued.

"Maybe not, but..."

Jim was interrupted when my cell phone rang.

"Don't answer it," he suggested.

I looked at the incoming number. "It's Marie," I told him. "Maybe she has news."

He sighed. "Fine."

I swiped the telephone symbol on my android phone to the right to answer, but before I could say anything, Marie beat me to it.

"Where are you?"

I lifted my eyebrows, and then realized that Marie couldn't see me. "Where are you?"

"I'm at The Mariner's Rest," she said, her tone indicating that she thought I should know that.

I thought for a second. "Oooh," I answered, drawing out the word.

"Yes. Oooh. We were supposed to meet for breakfast."

"Huh. I forgot."

"Clearly." She paused, and when no other information was forthcoming, she asked, "So, where are you?"

"We are currently standing outside the gates of the Sanctuary Park Cemetery," I answered.

It was her turn to be silent. "Why?" she finally inquired. "You didn't snap and kill Jim did you? I knew all that lovey dovey stuff couldn't last."

"Funny," I told her. "I thought it would be nice and quiet here."

"The crowds were bugging you that much?"

"I was getting tired of getting hurt."

"Ah, well, I can understand that." She paused again. "But why a cemetery?"

"Why not?" I answered. "People are dying to get in here, you know."

I was treated to groans from both Marie over the phone and Jim, standing beside me.

"Okay, that was pretty juvenile," I admitted. "I just thought I could get some neat pictures out here. You never know. Want to join us?"

Marie laughed. "Naw. I'm going to go over and get the results from the Sunday weigh offs."

"I got pictures of the biggest vegetables and pumpkins yesterday," I told her, "so all I'll need is a list of the winners for the article." I waited a beat before adding, "The cemetery seemed a safer choice."

She chuckled. "You're probably right on that count," she observed. "I will get the results for you. Do you two want to meet me for lunch?"

"Sure, at the Port in the Storm?"

"Sure," she echoed. "I hear Ilene is serving up everything left in her pantry that is remotely pumpkin based."

I laughed. "I will warn Jim. And I'm sorry about breakfast."

"No worries. See you in a while," Marie said before disconnecting.

"You will warn me about what?" Jim asked curiously.

"Marie said that Ilene will be serving whatever pumpkin edibles she has left for lunch," I answered. "Aren't you thrilled?"

"That's not exactly how I'd put it," he grumbled. He took my phone and pocketed it before I could grab it back. "No more phone calls," he said. "Remember, we came out here to decompress from all of the excitement."

"That's true," I agreed. "Okay, you can have my phone. For now."

He smiled and took my hand again as we headed towards the tall stone pillars that held up a beautiful cast iron gate at the entrance to the cemetery. We walked in on the road, which was lined with perfectly manicured cedar trees. We turned onto the first gravel-surfaced path that headed off into the tombstones, under the shade of multicoloured maple and other deciduous trees.

I took photos of various ornate tombstones and a few that indicated how married couples had passed within a short time of one another. Clearly the ones left behind unable to live without their spouses, a fact that I found sadly romantic. At one point of our exploration, a small hill rose up in front of us, dotted with tombstones of wide variety and age. They reached up into an increasingly cloudy sky, giving the entire view a decidedly spooky feel. I quickly took a photo.

"It's getting cooler," I observed.

"Wishful thinking," Jim said, wiping sweat from his brow.

I smiled indulgently at him. "Do you want to head back?"

"Do you have enough photos?"

I nodded.

"Decompressed enough?"

I nodded again.

"Well then, what are we waiting for?" He put his hands on my shoulders and turned me around. "Let's go!"

We headed back the way we came, careful to be respectful of any people we encountered that were leaving flowers at gravesides. As we approached the gates from the other side, I looked curiously across the road.

"What did Ilene call that place?" I pointed towards a large stand of trees facing the cemetery.

"The Pinery," Jim answered. "When you were in the washroom, she told me that she and her friends used to wander around in there as kids."

I snorted. "As kids, right. More like as teenagers, with partying involved."

"Why not both?"

"Why not indeed?" I agreed after a moment's thought.

We passed back through the gates to the cemetery and I stopped, staring at the small forested area. "The Pinery, you said.

Isn't that bound to get confused with the Pinery Provincial Park near Grand Bend?"

"I mentioned that to her. She said this one was there first."

"Makes sense, I guess." I crossed the road and squinted into the dense bush. "Do you see something orange back there?"

Jim joined me and squinted as well. "Where?"

I got closer to him so he could sight down my arm. "There."

He was quiet for so long that I was starting to lose my patience. "Maybe," he said finally, drawing out the word.

"Let's go check!"

"What?" he protested. "There isn't even a path through there."

"Doesn't matter," I declared, grabbing his hand and pulling him towards the dense underbrush.

"But why?" he questioned, very close to whining.

"Because," I told him. "I think we just found that giant metal pumpkin that I've been looking for!"

He squinted into the bush again. "Huh. If you say so." He pulled my cell phone out of his pocket. "Before we go in there, which looks like an accident waiting to happen by the way..."

I grabbed my phone from him and slapped his shoulder in response.

"...I want you to text Marie or Ilene or Myrna. Anyone really. Tell her where we are and what we're doing."

"Why would I want to do that?"

Jim shrugged. "Just in case something happens." He peered into the woods again, and as the sun passed behind a cloud, it looked more than a bit ominous. "It is us, after all."

I appreciated his effort to include himself in that statement when I knew what he really meant to say was that it was me who attracted trouble like hornets to Tim Horton's garbage bins in the fall. But I really didn't anticipate any problem at the moment.

"We're just taking a quick peek," I assured him. "Nothing is going to happen."

Jim let out a put-upon sigh. I hadn't realized until then how much he worried about me getting into trouble. "Wouldn't it be better to err on the safe side?" he asked.

I kissed his cheek. "I have you here with me," I told him. "What could possibly go wrong?" I put the phone away. "We can text them later if we need to."

Jim let out another sigh, accepting defeat.

"Shall we?" I asked, ignoring his suddenly sulkiness.

Jim offered me his arm. I slipped my hand through it, happy to know that no matter what crazy thing I wanted to do, my husband was willing to go along.

"We have a giant pumpkin to find!"

THE TRAVELLING KLUTZ

One of the joys of small town living is that, should you need information or directions, there are people more than willing to help you out.

Those from larger centres might think that it's impossible to get lost in a small town, but often smaller towns are spread out over a large geographical area and have an abundance of nook and crannies in which one can lose oneself. Truly, anywhere that is unfamiliar is simply an easy place to get lost.

The people of Port Elgin are a friendly lot, living up to their small town reputation. If you can't find a certain street, you need only stop the first person you meet and he or she will direct you to where you need to be. If you are looking for a certain store or restaurant, you will likely not only be told where to find it, but what to buy there and a short history of the business in question. If you can't find your way to the beach, harbour or campground, you can be sure that someone will give you the quickest way to get there, if not actually have you follow them there, so that they are certain you find it alright.

Of course, sometimes being in need of direction can bring you to spend time with some of those wonderful, small town people, perhaps over a meal or a beverage. And you will come away much the richer for the experience.

172

Chapter 16

It became abundantly clear fairly quickly that we were ill prepared for a trek through dense undergrowth. Within minutes we both bore red, angry scratches on our arms and legs from the thick branches and brush.

At least it wasn't jus me this time.

I stopped and looked at Jim. "What if there's poison ivy in here?" I worried.

He froze. "Perhaps we should rethink this, my sweet," he suggested.

I sighed. "As much as I want to find that giant pumpkin..."

"You ARE kind of like Ahab that way."

"...there might be a better way to attack this," I finished, refusing to take the bait.

Jim turned around, leading me back to the road. "Maybe Ilene knows of a better way in. She did say she hung out here as a kid."

"And maybe we can recruit a few other people to join us," I added.

"The more the merrier," he answered, his tone belying the sentiment. "At least we'll get some lunch."

We arrived back at the Mariner's Rest disheveled, scratched and sweaty. Just inside the door we encountered Myrna and Ilene, who were standing together behind the check-in desk, heads close as if they were up to no good.

"What happened to you two?" Myrna laughed when she saw us enter.

"What are you two up to?" I countered.

She narrowed her eyes. "That old trick doesn't work with me, missy."

"Missy? Gee, thanks! I haven't been called that for ages."

"For good reason," Jim mumbled.

"What was that?" I turned a scalding look at him.

"Nothing." He winked at the two women, who were coming out from behind the desk.

"You look like something the cat dragged in," Myrna declared, unwilling to let it go.

"A cat that put up quite a fight, by the looks of it," Ilene added. She turned to head back into the kitchen and motioned us all to follow.

We settled at the huge farm style table with sighs. Ilene removed a pitcher of ice water from the refrigerator and two large glasses from the cupboard beside the sink and placed them on the table. I poured each of us a glass. Neither of us said a word until we'd downed the entire serving of icy cold water and Jim had poured us a second glass.

"This," I waved a hand in front of the two of us, "is actually your fault Ilene."

She looked at us in surprise. "How could it possibly be my fault?"

"You suggested that we check out the Pinery," I explained.

"What did you do, roll about in it?" Myrna teased.

I looked at her. "We tried to walk through it."

"It's quite overgrown," Jim added.

"Why would you decide to go into the woods where there is no path?" Ilene asked, clearly puzzled.

"Because," I told her, "I thought I saw something orange."

"Wait," Myrna said. "This isn't making any sense at all. Start from the beginning."

"The beginning of what?"

We all turned to the kitchen door, where Marie was standing with a perplexed look on her face. "Now that I'm looking at you, I'd guess the beginning of the story as to why you look like you just survived a tornado."

Ilene snickered from the counter where she was preparing the day's lunch offerings.

"I'd like to hear that too," a deep voice boomed. Marie stepped into the room and Detective Wolsey filled the doorway.

"Ah great, the gang's all here!" Andrew quipped as he entered through a door off the side of the kitchen that led to the rooms set aside for Ilene as owner of the inn.

As we all settled in around the table, Ilene's serving staff whizzed in and out of the kitchen, serving lunch in the Port in the Storm cafe.

"Would you like us to go out into the cafe?" Marie asked.

"We're fine here," Ilene said with a wink. She then directed all of us in various chores, from setting the table to getting beverages to placing lunch items on the table family style.

There were two pumpkin-shaped tureens of pumpkin soup, one spicier than the other, baked pumpkin spice pretzels, the pumpkin hummus that we had enjoyed earlier with flatbread and crackers, and warm pumpkin bread with butter. Complimenting it all was a tray of cold meats and cheeses.

"Don't get too filled up," Ilene warned. "I have quite a few desserts that we have to eat up too."

"No danger of that," Wolsey said through a mouth full of bread.

"Ok," Marie said to us as she helped herself to some spicy soup, "'Fess up. What happened to you two?"

"We went over to the cemetery," I began.

"And there were zombies?" Andrew interrupted.

"Do you want to hear this or not?" I snapped.

"The floor is yours," he conceded.

177

"So, I took some photos at the cemetery while we wandered around in the peace and quiet."

"You never told me why you wanted those pictures," Marie pointed out.

I shrugged. "I'm thinking of doing a piece on Ontario cemeteries at some point," I told her. "It's just a thought."

"Not a bad one," she told me.

"Thanks! Anyway, when we left, we were checking out that Pinery woods that Ilene told us about..."

"I haven't been there in years," Myrna said. "Remember that time when we..."

Ilene shot her a warning look. "I believe Casey was telling us why they look like they got in a fight with a wildcat," she stated.

I looked at the two of them quizzically, but when nothing else was forthcoming, I continued. "And I saw something back in the woods. Something orange." I stressed the word orange.

"It is fall you know," Wolsey stated as he helped himself to a slice of cheese. "Are these bits of pumpkin seed in here?"

Ilene nodded before turning to me. "You say 'orange' like it means something specific."

I smiled, trying to look like I had a big secret, but probably coming across as someone with indigestion. "It does. Orange, as in something large, and metal."

They were all quiet for a moment, but it was Ilene's eyes that suddenly lit up with recognition. "You found the giant pumpkin!" she declared.

"I think so!" I exclaimed.

"You THINK so?" Marie asked, pushing away her empty plate with a satisfied sigh. "You're not sure?"

"Well, we headed into the woods to go see, but it was pretty overgrown..."

"Hence the scratches," Jim told them, unconsciously rubbing a scratch on his arm.

"And we thought that Ilene might know of a better spot to go in and look, so we came back," I concluded.

"Well that would be one mystery solved anyway," Ilene said as she stood to start cleaning the empty plates and bowls off of the table.

Wolsey scowled. "If that was a comment on the effectiveness of the police regarding this Cindy Citrouille case..." he began.

Ilene looked surprised at his outburst. "I assure you, Detective; it was nothing of the sort."

Marie had perked up at the mention of the missing woman. "How is that coming, anyway?" she asked him.

He frowned. "It isn't," he snapped. "There is nothing we can do. An adult has decided to go away without letting her friends know. That is allowed."

"I don't believe that," I stated.

"I'm aware of your feelings on the matter," he replied.

For a moment, the only sound was provided by Ilene's staff, which was busily plating desserts to take out to the cafe. Ilene and Myrna put the desserts left after that process onto the table, along with some mismatched plates, utensils, and coffee cups. Andrew pitched in by making a pot of coffee. I just sat and glared across the table at Wolsey, who gave as good as he got.

When Ilene and Myrna were done, the table was loaded with desserts. There was pumpkin crunch cake, a double layer pumpkin pie, pumpkin coconut cheesecake, an orange pumpkin cake and chocolate pumpkin cupcakes. I snagged a cupcake before they were all gone and put it on my plate.

"So, you want to know the best spot to get into the Pinery?" Ilene asked, relieving the silent tension around the table.

"The last spot was less than optimal," Jim conceded.

Ilene chuckled. "Clearly. There is a path off of Mill Street that you could try."

"Great!" I mumbled with my mouth full of cupcake. "These are good, by the way."

Ilene inclined her head in acknowledgement of the compliment.

"They can't be as good as this cheesecake," Marie argued, causing Ilene to smile in response.

"So," I said, draining my coffee and looking around the table at the motley crew I had gathered around me. "Who wants to go on an adventure?"

"There's pretty much nothing left for me to cover, so I might as well come along and see how many more scrapes and bruises you accumulate," Marie deadpanned, drawing laughter from everyone at the table.

"As much as I would enjoy seeing that," Wolsey said, "I have a meeting at the station to bring the chief up to speed on everything that happened this weekend. So I'm out." He turned to Marie. "Keep me on speed dial, though. Send video if it gets really interesting."

"Oh ye of little faith," I griped.

"Oh we of plenty of faith," Marie countered. "We have faith something will go wrong."

"And we would hate to miss it," Myrna added. She turned to Andrew. "What do you say? Should we go out in the muggy heat and traipse around looking for a mythical metal pumpkin or..." She left their other option to our imaginations.

Andrew grinned. "Well, since we are heading home tomorrow, I opt for the 'or'," he said, wiggling his eyebrows.

I stuck my fingers in my ears and sang "La, la, la" as loud as I could to drown out the rest of his answer. "TMI people!"

Ilene laughed. "You think Myrna's wild now, you should have seen her back in the day when our dance troupe was overseas..."

Myrna interrupted her. "They don't need to hear those old tales," she admonished.

"Oh I don't know, that sounds more interesting than whatever you two have planned," Jim teased.

"Point of view," Andrew replied, pulling Myrna to his side and kissing her cheek.

"On that note, adventure awaits," I declared. "Ilene? Come along and spill your secrets while we search?"

She chuckled. "I'll pass this time. Happy hunting."

THE TRAVELLING KLUTZ

When you are a resident of a small town, such as Port Elgin, you can always count on running into someone you know. Whether you are at a large event such as Pumpkinfest, or just out strolling down the main street, or shopping at Walmart, you shouldn't be surprised when you run into a person with whom you are acquainted.

Even as someone who had lived in Kincardine, a half an hour's drive south of town, we were always surprised when we ran into others from our town taking advantage of the shopping or special events that Port Elgin offered. And when you run into someone you know, it is inevitable that you stop and have at least a brief chat with the person in question. Part of that is due to the outgoing friendliness of small towns in general, and part is just plain old small town manners.

No place in town is exempt from this basic rule. You are bound to run into someone you know no matter where you wander.

Of course, sometimes it's just the worst bit of luck that you run into the last person you want to see. Even if you didn't know you didn't want to see that person until it was too late.

Chapter 17

The three of us piled into our car and drove to Mill Street, which bisected the wood lot, with a slightly smaller swath of trees to the north and the larger section to the south of the street. We parked near the water tower over at the end of the road. Just as Ilene had told us, there was a rough path into the Pinery woods on both sides of the street.

"I wish we had known about these paths earlier," Jim groused.

"Well, we know now!" I said in the cheeriest voice I could muster. I looked at our options. "The cemetery is that way, right?" I pointed into the northern swath of trees.

Jim nodded in confirmation.

"So, the orange we saw would likely be in this area, right?" I reasoned. "There's no way we could have spotted something through these trees, across the road, and into those trees. Is there?"

"It is highly unlikely," he concurred.

"Could it just have been some of the leaves turning orange?" Marie asked. "Because now that I'm here, I'm surprised you were able to see anything at all through that thick bush." She gestured at the area surrounding the path. It was thick with undergrowth and difficult to see through, but the path was clear and ventured surely into the dense woods.

I shook my head. "I know what I saw," I told her. "It was a different shade of orange than fall leaves."

"You're sure?"

I paused. "Fairly," I answered.

Marie shook her head in amusement. "So we go this way then?" she asked, already moving towards the path.

"Wait! Why don't I go this way, Jim can go around and approach it from Eastwood Drive and Marie can go to the other side through the water tower yard?" I looked at their confused expressions. "Then we can meet up on the path halfway through."

"You want to split up?" Jim asked, his voice sounding alarmed.

I shrugged. "I'll stay on the trail," I tried to placate him. "There will be less chance of me getting in trouble on such a nice, flat surface."

"Famous last words," Marie muttered.

"What was that?"

She looked up at the sky. "Nothing."

I shook my head and turned back to my husband. "Come on, sweetie," I cajoled. "It's not that big of a woodlot. We'll be within shouting distance of each other." I looked over and saw Marie fiddling with her phone. "What are you doing?" I asked, suspicion sneaking into my tone.

"Getting my phone set up to call our favourite detective," she informed me.

I gritted my teeth. "We won't NEED to call Wolsey," I told her. "We're just looking for a big metal pumpkin. What could go wrong?"

"Again," Marie said pointedly. "Famous. Last. Words." She looked at me, her eyes dancing with amusement. "Did I say it loud enough for you to hear this time?"

"Funny," I grumbled.

Jim pulled out his phone. "You're right, Marie. I'm going to get 911 cued up and ready to go."

Marie laughed at the dismayed look on my face. She turned to Jim. "Have you ever considered getting her a dog?" she asked. "That way, she wouldn't be alone."

"I think I serve that purpose," he joked.

"You're probably right," Marie conceded, still chuckling. "How about a bell? Have you thought of putting a bell on her?"

Jim chuckled this time. "I invite you to try," he deadpanned.

I looked from one to the other of them as they continued the let's-bash-Casey routine.

"Maybe if you made it look like a piece of jewelry," Marie suggested.

"Hmmm, I will have to look into that."

In equal measures of exasperation and amusement, I rolled my eyes and headed for the trail. "I'll see you both on the

187

other side," I told the two jokesters, not even bothering to look back to see if they were actually going to follow my plan.

I was surprised at how quickly I was swallowed up by trees. I looked around furtively, suddenly doubting the wisdom of my decision to go it alone. I turned around, hoping to see Jim or Marie or both walking behind me, but there was sadly no sign of them.

They just had to choose this time to do something I asked.

With a shrug, I turned back and scanned the surrounding trees for any hint of orange. Was it possible that I hadn't really seen anything earlier?

No, I couldn't believe that. The leaves were falling; perhaps the giant pumpkin, or whatever else orange that was out there, had been covered up. I nodded, congratulating myself on such a feat of logic, and continued down the path.

After a few minutes of scanning in front and to both sides, I thought that I saw a flash of orange ahead and to the right. If she had followed the plan, Marie would be approaching from the right. If I headed towards the tiny bright spot of colour, I'd likely run into her.

"Hello?" I called out. I waited for a response from Marie, but none came. I shrugged; telling myself that she likely hadn't had time to even enter the woods yet, having had to circle to the side. After looking unenthusiastically at the underbrush, acutely feeling every scratch on my body from earlier, I squinted at the orange spot and made my decision.

I left the path and headed through the underbrush to find the pumpkin.

Oddly enough, it wasn't as rough going as our attempt earlier in the day. It was almost as if there was a rough trail, possibly created by animals or curious children.

"This isn't so bad," I said aloud as I cautiously progressed. "Great, now I'm talking to myself."

I shook my head as I continued along the rough trail, getting a few scratches on my legs but nothing like the number the two of us had accrued earlier. I squinted at the area I had zeroed in on and was sure I could see a small bit of orange, at about the four foot high level. *Surely, that's too low to be the orange of changing leaves*, I thought.

"Stop calling yourself Shirley," I told myself out loud, chuckling at the old joke from the movie Airplane.

Suddenly the dense brush gave way to a slight clearing. I almost stumbled when I encountered the sudden lack of resistance. I caught myself on a sapling and looked in surprise, triumph, and slight confusion at the area before me.

It was definitely the giant metal pumpkin that I had been looking for all weekend. But only a small bit of it was showing. The entire 7 foot tall, ball-shaped structure was covered in branches. It didn't look like those branches had just fallen on the pumpkin either. They seemed to be strategically placed over the top and leaning onto the sides of the metal gourd, concealing it almost entirely from view. The entrance to the inside was completely obscured, and I realized that had it not been for that small piece of side where a branch had succumbed to gravity and fallen away, I would never have spotted the flash of orange that I had seen.

"Well, that's just odd," I said to myself.

I approached the structure cautiously, running through possible explanations for it being camouflaged in such a way. Clearly, someone was trying to hide it, but why?

The first possibility that popped into my head was that kids had done this. Either it was a club house for a bunch of boys, lacking only the 'no girls allowed' sign, and hidden from view when they were not in attendance. Or, as Ilene had mentioned previously, it was serving as a party spot for teenagers, far from prying adult eyes, and they had hidden it to keep it secret.

Either way, if I wanted a good picture of it, I would have to pull all of the branches off. And that would likely upset someone who had gone to a lot of trouble to put them there in the first place. I pulled out my phone to take a picture of it as it was, prepared to turn around and meet Jim and Marie at the end of the trail. As I took the picture, I thought I heard a sound coming from the middle of the metal pumpkin.

I lowered my phone and cocked my head to the side to listen. That was when I heard the sound of a footstep behind me. I froze, chills running up and down my spine, as I realized that I was about to regret that decision to split up. *Jim is going to be so mad,* I thought.

"I really wish you hadn't seen this," a familiar voice said, just before stars exploded in my eyes and everything went black.

As in most small towns, Port Elgin's Public Library is considered by many to be the heart of the community. Not only is it an architectural treasure, it is also an irreplaceable resource for residents and visitors alike.

Built in 1908, the landmark building which houses the library is one of the few remaining Carnegie Libraries. Carnegie libraries were built thanks to donations from Scottish philanthropist Andrew Carnegie. A staunch believer in the importance of libraries, Carnegie has been quoted as saying, "There is not such a cradle of democracy upon the earth as the Free Public Library, this republic of letters, where neither rank, office, nor wealth receives the slightest consideration."

A total of 1,689 libraries were built around the world, with 125 of those constructed in Canada, the majority in the province of Ontario. Of the 111 libraries built in Ontario, only 65 remain operating, including the one in Port Elgin. In fact five of those functioning libraries, located in Kincardine, Lucknow, Port Elgin, Teeswater, and Walkerton, all fall under the Bruce County Public Library umbrella.

The majestic red brick, two storied building, located on Port Elgin's Goderich Street, has been upgraded in recent years with an eye to restoring its original architecture while allowing increased accessibility. It features large windows on each floor, a centrally located main entrance where a stairway sits between two sets of two white columns. In addition to a wide variety of books, both hardcover and paperback, the library offers magazines, newspapers, videos, DVDs, puzzles, public access computers and wireless internet access. It also features various programs for adults and children, making it an essential part of the community.

No matter who you are, you can go to the library for inspiration in your life.

Of course, there is always the chance that the wrong person could be inspired in the least desirable of ways.

Chapter 18

I have the worse migraine ever, I thought with a groan.

I reached up to rub my temple, only to realize that for some reason, I was doing so with both my hands. Anticipating the searing pain that comes with opening one's eyes to bright light during a migraine, I cautiously cracked an eyelid to see what was up with my hands.

Both eyes flew open then and I didn't even register the dim light as I stared at my hands, currently tied together with rough brown twine.

"What the...?" At least that's what I tried to say, but it just came out as a shocked mumble. My mouth tasted like my lunch had tried to work its way up out of my stomach and I tried to spit.

Which led to the realization that, not only were my hands tied, but I was gagged as well.

I looked down at my hands again, which were remarkably tied in front of my body. Despite the pounding in my head, I quickly wondered who would be stupid enough to gag someone and then tie her hands IN FRONT of her. The eye roll I attempted was aborted immediately due to the pain it engendered, and I lifted my hands back up to my head. Determining that there was duct tape over my mouth, I steeled myself for some more pain and yanked the sticky tape off of my mouth as though I was tearing off a bandage.

I'd have cursed at that point, but I still had to pull whatever was inside my mouth out. Grabbing hold of something that felt distinctly like silk, I pulled the obstruction free and squinted at it in the dim light.

Only to immediately drop what looked suspiciously like a pair of men's boxer shorts.

"Bloody hell," I whispered through my dry mouth, borrowing my favourite detective's favourite saying. I didn't want to ponder whether this pair of underwear was clean or not.

Turning to the twine on my hands, I found the knot on the underside of my wrists and spent the next few minutes trying to get hold of part of it with my teeth. After a few failed attempts, I managed to loosen the knot and pull the twine from my red and painfully pulsing wrists.

Only then did I take the time to look around. I really should have done that first, but I'd been hit on the head. That was my excuse and I was sticking to it.

The first thing I noticed was that I was in a stifling hot, circular structure. The walls were steel grey and arced upwards towards a centre point on the ceiling. My muddled brain mulled that over for a minute before coming up with the obvious answer to where I currently found myself.

I was inside the giant metal pumpkin.

"Yay me," I mumbled. "I found it."

I froze as a muffled response came from the other side of the room. Squinting, I could just make out a shape in the gloom. Fear rushed through me like a heat wave.

Who knew that a giant pumpkin with no windows and covered in brush would be so dark inside?

A louder mumble, accompanied by what sounded like the rattling of chains, had me scooting backwards until I was backed against the wall. I looked frantically for the door, but in the darkness it refused to show itself.

The sounds across from me started to sound more like sobs. After considering my options, which I decided were few, I opted to check out the dark shape. I reached into my pocket for my phone, thinking to use the flashlight, and then very nearly hit myself on the forehead in exasperation as I realized that I should have gone for it as soon as I was free. Luckily, I remembered my aching head just in time and refrained.

But there would be no call for help or flashlight, because my phone wasn't there. I must have dropped it when...

"Son of a witch!" I hissed. "He hit me on the head!"

The shape across from me momentarily forgotten, I tried to remember just who had knocked me out. When the memory wasn't immediately forthcoming, I did what I always did when I couldn't remember something. I put the question aside for my brain to 'percolate', and decided to find out what or who else was inside the pumpkin with me.

Not that I really wanted to, but there was nothing for it. I was expecting a trapped animal. What I found chilled me to the bone.

As I got nearer to the shape, it was suddenly clear that it was a person. I moved forward more quickly now and saw a woman, hands and feet chained, and another chain leading from what I assumed was a leather collar to a sturdy loop attached to the wall.

"Oh my god!" I cried, and the woman shook her head urgently, a sound like a hiss coming from her. She was clearly trying to shush me, and I nodded that I understood.

I got closer and saw that she had also been gagged, but whoever had done this to her had done a much better job of it than had been done to me. The apparatus resembled the ones I had seen on the television show *A Handmaid's Tale*. Made of leather, a pouch of sorts went under the woman's chin and over the entire lower side of her face, barely leaving her nose open from breathing. It was held in place by leather straps that went behind her head both under and over her ears.

I reached behind her head, something I saw she wouldn't have been able to do as her hands were tied with very little leeway to her feet. Then I cursed under my breath. The straps ended in metal loops, which were fastened together with a sturdy, metal lock.

"I can't get it," I whispered. "It's locked."

Her eyes filled with tears that I could barely see in the gloom and she whimpered. Now that my eyes were adjusting to the gloom, I could see that her clothes - a pair of shorts and a tank top - were torn in places and filthy, like she'd rolled about in the mud at some point. The only clean spots on her were where sweat had made trails through the dirt on her skin. There were dark marks around her wrists and ankles, where leather cuffs were also locked closed around links of chain. I realized the darkness was blood and I shuddered. I looked into her eyes with sympathy, and when I did so, the light came on in my head.

Because I knew those eyes. The last time I'd seen them, they had been flashing in anger after their owner had tossed a pair of boxer shorts on my head.

Not only had I found the giant pumpkin, I had found Cindy as well.

"Cindy?" I whispered.

She nodded, and then looked to the left into the darkness.

I gasped. "It was Pierre! He said something just before he hit me!"

She nodded again, tears threatening to overflow. She pointedly looked from me to the same side of the room again.

"We have to get out of here!" I whispered urgently.

She held up her hands, rattling the chains gently, and shrugged. She wasn't going anywhere locked up as she was. She wanted me to go without her.

I wasn't ready to do that just yet. "Is there anything in here that we can cut the cuffs with?" I wondered.

She shook her head, the sadness in her eyes speaking volumes that she could not give voice to. She stared at me, and then jerked her head at the far wall.

"The door is there?"

She nodded.

"I can't leave you here," I told her.

"You won't have to," Pierre said as he opened the door, letting some light in and blinding us momentarily. I flinched at the sound of anger in his voice and placed myself between him and his wife. "We are all going to get out of here, together," he said ominously.

The light was dim behind Pierre and I briefly wondered how long I had been unconscious. Then I realized that while I could see better thanks to the light coming in through the open door and silhouetting Pierre's form, his eyesight was likely still adjusting to the decrease of light inside the pumpkin.

It was now or never, I realized. No doubt looking braver than I felt, I rushed at him; taking advantage of what I hoped was his temporary blindness. My goal was to knock him down and run away, screaming the entire time. I would find Jim and Marie and they would contact Wolsey and the 911 operator. The police would come and rescue Cindy and arrest Pierre. It was the perfect, on the spot plan.

But, considering who had come up with that plan, it was no surprise when it failed miserably.

I ran at him, and he didn't see me coming until it was too late. That part worked like a charm, and had it been implemented by anyone else, that person would be sprinting through the trees towards safety right now.

Unfortunately, it was implemented by me. Just before I crashed into Pierre, my foot came down on the pair of boxer shorts I had removed from my mouth and tossed away from me in disgust minutes before. My foot slipped out from under me, lashing out behind me like a donkey kick, and I fell forward.

Right into Pierre's waiting arms. Not that he came away unscathed. My momentum made sure of that.

I hit him with my full weight and he fell backwards. His arms wrapped around me tightly and I went down as well, right on top of him. He landed with an audible 'oof', but he continued to hold onto me despite having had all of his air knocked out of him. I struggled fiercely, getting a few head blows and wild kicks in, but it quickly became clear that my 55-year-old self was no match for a young, fit man.

He grabbed a handful of my hair and his other hand wrapped roughly around my sore wrist. He pushed me to the side before rising, yanking me to my feet with him as he rose.

"You are a menace!" he growled at me.

"I've heard that before," I mouthed off at him, clearly not thinking straight, "and from better men than you."

He let go of my hair and backhanded me across the face. I fell to the ground and stayed there, my head ringing with what seemed like a warm up for a bell wringers orchestra before a Christmas performance of Carol of the Bells. And then, for the second time that day, I passed out.

THE TRAVELLING KLUTZ

If, after your visit to Port Elgin, you are inspired to relocate there permanently, rest assured that the town and the greater municipality of Saugeen Shores is not only a safe place to visit, but to live as well.

The area is well served by a volunteer fire department of 50 dedicated firefighters. Those highly skilled volunteers work out of two fire stations, one on Emma Street in Port Elgin and the other on Victoria Street South in Southampton, assuring optimum coverage for the area. The department is supported by a fire chief, a fire prevention officer and an administrative assistant.

The Ambulance Service is provided by the County of Bruce Paramedic Services, which has a staff of 100 highly trained paramedics and a fleet of 12 ambulances and 3 supervisor units. The service provides timely medical and trauma care to citizens and visitors alike.

Saugeen Shores is one of the few municipalities in the area to still have its own police services, instead of contracting out to the Ontario Provincial Police for its law enforcement needs. The Saugeen Shores Police Service has 21 full time and 4 part time officers, as well as 6 auxiliary officers and 3 civilian staff members. The department, located on Tomlinson Drive in Port Elgin, covers an area of just over 170 kilometres, including 432 kilometres of roads. They are dedicated to keeping the people of Saugeen Shores safe and secure.

No matter what kind of help you need, you can rest assured that it is only a quick call away, whether you are visiting or living in Port Elgin.

Unfortunately, some people seem to need emergency services more often than others.

Chapter 19

I came to in the back seat of an SUV with blacked out windows. The bad news was that my hands were tied again; this time behind my back. The good news was that I was alone. It was hot and stuffy in the vehicle and sweat dripped into my eyes. I blinked and looked around to be sure that no one was nearby.

I assumed that Pierre had gone to get his wife. I realized that I didn't have much time to do something to improve my situation and to help Cindy. I didn't like the possibilities that were running through my mind of what would happen should I still be tied up in the back seat when Pierre returned.

I looked around the vehicle, considering my options. I could get into the front seat and lean on the horn. But the odds of me being able to get over the high back of the front seat, with my hands tied, without getting hurt in the process, were slim at best. Besides, blowing the horn might only succeed in drawing Pierre's attention to my efforts, and that was the last thing I wanted. By that logic, screaming at the top of my lungs, in hopes of getting help, was likely a bad idea as well.

I could try to get my hands in front of me by bringing them around my rear end and feet. I had seen hostages perform that move on television a few times. At the thought of me trying to perform such intricate acrobatics in the cramped back seat, I chuckled despite my dismal situation and quickly dismissed the idea.

I could try to get the door open using my feet or mouth or bound hands or any combination thereof. I eyeballed the door handle for a moment and decided that was the most likely course of action to take.

I couldn't tell if the door was locked or not. I just hoped that Pierre didn't have the child-proof locks activated. Because if he did, I would have to try getting into the front seat after all, and I really didn't want to try that plan.

I turned my back to the door and shimmied up to it. I was glad there was no one watching, because I was certain it wasn't a pretty picture. Then again, if someone was watching I wouldn't be in this predicament.

You wouldn't be in this predicament if you hadn't insisted on splitting up, I silently scolded myself. *Stupid, stupid, stupid.*

I silently wished that it were Jim scolding me right now.

My fingers kept slipping off of the slick, cool metal of the door handle. I figured they were sweaty, but I stubbornly refused to give up. I kept glancing out the window in fear, dreading the iminent return of Pierre. After a while the handle seemed to be more on the sticky side than slick, and that actually seemed to help my finger tips get a grip. Finally, when my fingers were cramping painfully and I was about to collapse in exhaustion against the door, I managed to grasp the end of the handle and pull the lever to open the door.

I clearly hadn't thought this through.

The door opened, but the problem was that I was leaning heavily on it when it did. I tumbled out of the SUV like a bunch of garbage tossed carelessly outside. I landed heavily on my back, knocking my breath out of my lungs and narrowly preventing another blow to my head. My legs were up in the air and my feet were propped up on the back seat. Feeling like a cartoon character from my childhood, I shook my aching head to clear it. Then I struggled to get my feet under me and stand.

I banged into the door and the vehicle more times than I planned to admit if I ever got the chance to recount the tale of my oh-so-daring escape. Finally, after a copious amount of twisting, turning and swearing under my breath, I got my feet under me. I leaned against the vehicle and eased slowly into a standing position, pausing to peek through the windows to see if Pierre was about to wallop me again.

Seeing that the coast was clear, I wasted no time high tailing it away from the area. I could only hope that I was running in the right direction, as I had no idea where I was in relation to my previous location. I saw a path through the woods and, since I knew the pumpkin had been off the main path, I careened down it frantically.

I was feeling pretty good about my escape until I rounded a bend and ran head first into what felt like a cushy wall. I felt myself falling backwards once again and, without my hands to break my fall, I knew that this was going to hurt. I scrunched my eyes closed in anticipation of the impact.

A strong arm snaked around my waist and pulled me upright. I opened my eyes, relief and fear rushing through me in equal measure, unsure as to whom I would be face to face with, and terrified that it would be Pierre.

Wolsey put his hands on my waist and lifted me up, depositing me behind him on the path as though I weighed no more than a toddler. I have to admit, I was impressed at this feat of strength. He put a finger to his lips in warning. "Shhhh."

You could have knocked me over with a feather.

When another pair of arms circled me from behind and held me tight, I sagged back and sighed with relief. "You just took years off of my life, my sweet," Jim whispered in my ear.

As he set about untying my hands, I saw Wolsey jerk his head, indicating that Jim should get me out of there. Jim had managed to loosen the bonds, but he apparently saw the same urgency as the detective and he turned me around and, supporting me with an arm around the waist, guided me away from the area. We passed a number of uniformed officers on the way, including the now familiar young man who seemed to be part of the cleanup crew for all of my misadventures in Port Elgin, hurrying towards Wolsey's position.

Once we were out of sight and earshot, Jim stopped and tackled the bonds again. My fingers were numb by the time he released me. I cried out softly as my fingers began to tingle and blood returned to them.

"Damn it," he muttered, still on the quiet side.

I looked down at what had made him curse and gasped. My hands were covered with blood. Apparently, all of that struggling had caused the twine to break the skin.

"Let's go over to the paramedics and get this looked at," he whispered, his face a storm cloud of anger. "There's an ambulance waiting at the end of the path."

I followed him meekly. "But how did you know I was here?" I asked.

He hugged me close. "All in good time, my sweet."

206

It turned out that 'all in good time' was a lot longer than I anticipated.

We reached the ambulance and two paramedics whisked me away to be bandaged, poked and prodded.

"It looks like she has a mild concussion," the young blonde man who had been shining a bright penlight in my eyes for the last five minutes told Jim.

"Hello," I said, waving my hand in front of his face. I was momentarily distracted by the white bandages on my wrists that, combined with the bandage on my hand from earlier, made me look like a mummy. But I quickly returned my attention to the paramedic. "I'm right here."

Jim grabbed my hand and brought it to his lips, making me immediately feel guilty about my outburst.

"I'm sorry," I told him. "I should never have gone off alone."

"No, you shouldn't have."

"But how did you find me?"

"Technically," Jim teased, "you found us."

I was about to argue the point when a commotion inside the woods drew our attention. Wolsey emerged a second later, hauling a handcuffed Pierre out of the woods. For his part, Pierre was muttering what I assumed was a string of curses in French and struggling against the detective. Wolsey looked like he would like nothing more that to cuff the younger man in an entirely different way.

For once, I was rooting for the detective.

"We need a stretcher back there," he barked. "Female, mid-twenties, dehydrated and traumatized, but otherwise ok."

"That would be Cindy," I told Jim.

"We figured," he answered as the paramedics nudged me out of their way and headed down the path with their equipment atop of a gurney.

"But HOW?" I demanded.

Jim smiled. "Let's get back to the Mariner's Rest and catch everyone up at once," he suggested.

"Shouldn't we be going to the police station?"

"They know where to find us," he insisted. "You need to rest."

I knew when I was beat. Plus my head hurt too much to argue, and I was exhausted. I let him lead me to our car.

"I WILL get the whole story from you," I warned him.

He kissed my forehead. "Ditto, my sweet."

A sign of a warm and welcoming people is that, when it's time to say farewell, you are not enthused to do so.

Small towns often affect people in that manner, and the town of Port Elgin is no different in that regard. It isn't just the locations, such as the beach, the B&B, and the restaurants that make you wish you could stay. Nor is it just the activities you've enjoyed, such as Pumpkinfest and the large number of smaller events that make it up. Those are definitely part of the feeling that you will hold fondly in your memories as you return home or travel elsewhere.

But it is the people who leave an indelible mark on you. And it's not only the friendly people who took the time to give you directions, or the wait staff who took the time to accommodate you despite being super busy at the time. It's also the plethora of volunteers you encounter at the events you have come to enjoy and the workers where you have temporarily hung your hat, who go above and beyond to ensure that you have a wonderful stay.

And for some people it is the police officers and paramedics who have cared for you, some more than once, when you have had the odd mishap.

Some people just can't seem to stay out of trouble, after all.

Chapter 20

I was surprised when I had barely managed to wash up and change my clothes before I heard Detective Wolsey's booming voice a full two stories below me.

"Where is she? We need to get her statement."

I could barely hear Jim's voice reply, an indication of how urgent the detective thought his visit was.

Did he not have anyone else to harass?

I sighed and limped my way towards the stairs. When we had first arrived in town, I had been thrilled to get the third floor turret room and had marvelled at the grandeur of the staircase. Now, as my entire body ached and my head pounded relentlessly around what had initially been golf ball sized lump until Pierre's second blow had helped it grow to a tennis ball sized one, I had an entirely different opinion of navigating the stairs now. I stood at the top, held the handrail in a death grip, and steeled myself for a painful descent.

Luckily, my muscles loosened up with every step, so that by the time I got to the bottom I was barely hobbling at all.

"There you are, hobble-along Cassidy," Marie teased.

Ok, maybe I was hobbling worse than I thought.

Jim came over and offered me his arm, which I took gratefully. We followed Marie past the front desk and towards the kitchen.

"Wolsey is in a snit," she warned me.

"I heard, from three floors up."

"And he has company," she added. "They want all of our statements."

I sighed. "At least they're letting us do it here."

"I didn't give them a choice," Jim growled. "You have a concussion."

"Just a small one," I said, holding up my thumb and index finger in a demonstration, trying to make light of the situation. "Teeny tiny, really."

"Whatever. If it gets too much for you, I'm pulling the plug."

"My hero." I squeezed his hand.

"Always," he confirmed warmly, kissing my cheek.

"Gah!" Marie complained. "Give it a rest." For once, she didn't really sound too upset about our show of affection.

I chuckled softly, trying to keep the noise down for the sake of my head. "Who else is here?" I asked, hesitating at the door to the kitchen. It seemed to be pretty noisy in there and I suddenly wanted to turn around and go back to our room.

"Wolsey, of course," Marie answered. "And his little police buddy who will be writing down everything you say. Ilene, because it's her place after all. Myrna and Andrew. Cindy, Lori, Helen, and Velma, who are pretty much joined at the hips at the moment. And the three of us will make an even dozen."

I sighed, anticipating a lot of noise. "It doesn't sound like I have a snowball's chance of a quiet interview," I lamented. I straightened my back and threw back my shoulders in determination. "Well, let's get this over with," I said, striding into the room.

The chatter around the table ceased entirely when I entered. Maybe this wouldn't be so bad after all.

They all stared at me for a moment. Just as I was starting to feel self conscious, Cindy eased out of her seat and grabbed me in such an enthusiastic hug that I almost fell over. Luckily, Jim was standing behind me and, with a hand on each of my shoulders, steadied me so I could awkwardly return the young woman's embrace.

She pulled back and looked me in the eyes. "You saved me," she declared. "I can never thank you enough."

Her second hug brought a grunt of pain from me and she instantly jumped back. "I'm so sorry!"

I smiled at her. "Don't worry about it," I reassured her. "I'm used to the bumps and bruises."

"Ain't that the truth," Wolsey grumbled. "Are you ready to tell us how you got into trouble this time?"

I frowned at him. "Are you ready to hear it?" I countered. "I TOLD you Cindy was missing, but you wouldn't believe me."

"Oh come on!" he exclaimed. "You were out there looking for that damn pumpkin. You had no idea she was out there."

He had me there. "Wrong place, right time," I countered, although it sounded weak even to my own ears.

Jim chuckled and pulled out a chair for me. I eased into it, groaning at the pain in my head, back, arms, wrists, and shins. He planted a soothing kiss on the top of my head and sat beside me.

Ilene placed a huge mug in front of me. It was emblazoned with the words 'Pumpkin Spice Princess' in large orange letters, with smaller black letters beneath that read "Now bow down peasant'. The steam rising from the mug smelled like a combination of gingerbread and peppermint. I smiled up at her. "This smells like Christmas," I observed in surprise.

She smiled back and put a gentle hand on my shoulder. "Ginger and peppermint tea have been known to help with headaches," she told me.

She stepped aside as I thanked her and took my first delicious sip. When I looked up, Myrna had taken her place. She handed me a bag of frozen peas.

"Also for your head," she declared, before returning to her seat. With a wince, I put the peas against what in my mind seemed to have become a grapefruit sized lump since I had left my room and struggled down the stairs.

"Are we ready now?" Wolsey growled impatiently.

I nodded and sipped more tea.

"Good. First things first. I'd like to introduce the officer who will be recording all of your statements today." He indicated a young man sitting beside him.

The officer, the same one we had seen at the hot dog cart dumping, the alpaca attack and at the rescue operation, was about 28 years old, dark haired and big boned. He clearly worked hard at the gym to keep himself fit. He smiled and an adorable dimple appeared on one side of his face.

"This is Officer Cameron Wolsey," the detective said quickly.

I looked up suddenly, instantly regretting it as I saw flashes in front of my eyes. I looked at the detective and raised my eyebrows. It was less painful than asking my question out loud.

He sighed, knowing what I wanted to ask. "Yes, we are related," he admitted. "Cam is my son."

As I was digesting this nugget and realizing that no one else seemed surprised, the young man spoke up. "I've heard all about you," he told me in a smooth, baritone voice, his eyes briefly twinkling with mischief.

I sighed. "I'm sure you have, Junior."

The younger Wolsey frowned. "That would be Officer Wolsey to you," he growled.

"Oh how cute," Marie drawled. "Junior has the same attitude as the De-tec-tive."

That remained to be seen. Unlike his father, Junior seemed to know when to choose his battles. He opted to ignore us and turned his attention to the pad of paper on the table in front of him.

"Alright, let's start at the beginning," Wolsey said, nodding to Wolsey Junior. "Cindy, whenever you're ready. Just keep in mind that someone is writing down what you say, so try not to go too fast."

Beside me, I saw Marie subtly turn on her tiny tape recorder. Luckily, everyone's attention was on Cindy and no one saw me smile.

Cindy nodded and took a drink of water before beginning her tale. "After I spoke to you down at the police station, Detective, I headed back to my apartment. I had a bit of a mess to clean up."

"Yes, we saw that," Lori told her. "It scared us."

Wolsey glared at the young woman, and she instantly looked contrite.

"What happened next?" Wolsey prodded, sensitive to the fact that Cindy was clearly upset by the memories she was reliving. Her hands were shaking and her face had gone white.

Would wonders never cease? I thought.

"I was in the stairway leading up to my apartment," she told us, "when I heard someone coming up the stairs behind me." She paused and took another drink, the water sloshing over the side of the glass slightly.

"Take your time," Wolsey said, sounding sympathetic. I pinched myself to make sure I wasn't dreaming.

"Before I could turn around, someone put a cloth over my face," Cindy continued. "It smelled kind of sweet, in a chemical way, if that makes sense."

Wolsey nodded. "Chloroform," he confirmed, nodding at Junior to write that down as well.

"I must have passed out," Cindy said. Her eyes filled with tears. "When I woke up, I was chained to the wall of a round room. My hands and feet were chained too. I started to scream, but it was so hot in there that I was having trouble breathing. No one came, and I had to force myself to calm down, to get my breathing under control. I didn't have an inhaler!"

I sympathized with her, knowing all too well what it was like to have your airways close up on you.

"Then Pierre came in," she said, tears escaping and running down her cheeks. "I was still mad at him, but I was so happy to see him at that point." She looked around the table at all of us. "I thought he was there to save me."

She hung her head, clearly embarrassed at the admission.

"But he wasn't, was he?" Wolsey prodded after a moment.

She shook her head. Andrew offered her an actual linen handkerchief and she took it with a sad smile. She looked a bit puzzled as to whether she should actually use it, but once Andrew nodded at her, she blew her nose, and then continued her tale. "He tossed me an inhaler that he must have taken from my pocket. I used up the last of the medicine. He still hadn't said anything and I asked him to get me out of there before whoever took me returned."

"What did he say?" Marie, who was taking notes as quickly as Junior, asked.

Wolsey frowned at the interruption but didn't complain. I thought that he must be on his best behaviour to set an example for his son.

Cindy shuddered. "He laughed!" Her eyes welled up again. "He laughed at me! And THEN I realized what had happened. That HE had taken me, and my stomach just dropped. I felt sick."

"Did he say why?" I asked her, figuring that since Marie had gotten away with asking a question, I might as well try it too.

Wolsey looked like he was grinding his teeth to keep from exploding, but he remained quiet.

Cindy nodded in my direction. "He said that he would never let me leave him," she answered. "He said that I was HIS wife and I would always be his wife. He said that if I wouldn't behave like his wife, then he would keep me there until I came to my senses."

"What happened then?" Wolsey asked gently.

She looked like she was about to burst into tears. "I screamed. I figured that someone might hear me and come to help me. I didn't know where I was and I figured with the town so full of people, someone was bound to hear me."

"But no one did," I whispered.

She shook her head, the tears beginning to flow. "He freaked," she continued. "He pulled out that contraption, that thing that looked like it was a prop from *The Handmaid's Tale* on

218

TV. " She blew her nose again, her hands shaking. "He put a cloth in my mouth and then locked that cover around my head."

We all sat silent as that statement hung in the air. After a moment, Wolsey asked, "Would you like to take a break?"

Cindy wiped her eyes with trembling hands and shook her head. "I'd like to get this over with," she said. She took a deep breath to centre herself and then, her voice shaky, she continued. "He would take it off for me to eat, and he'd take me outside to go to the bathroom every now and then. The first time he took me outside was when I realized that we were nowhere near anyone. It felt so hopeless. I had another asthma attack. He was furious when he realized that he'd need to get me some more inhalers."

"Did he?"

She nodded. "I don't know where he got one. I figured that someone would be watching my place by that point, and he couldn't very well renew my prescription. But somehow he got one."

"I think I have an idea where it came from," I said dryly, remembering how he had picked up my camera bag when I'd accidentally left it behind on the trails during that first search for Cindy.

She looked at me, puzzled.

"He took one of mine," I explained to her.

"Well then you saved me twice," she stammered, her eyes filling up again with tears. Silently, she reached over and squeezed my less injured hand. After a moment, she continued

219

her story. "I don't know how much time went by, but it went on the same way until one time he came in and dumped someone else in the room. The person," she looked at me, "was unconscious. There were no more chains so he just tied the person up and left." She looked at Wolsey then. "Casey woke up a while later; I'm not sure how long it was. I thought I might actually get rescued when she charged at him like she did."

"You did what now?" Jim asked in surprise.

They all turned and looked at me. I just shrugged.

"Well, Casey," Wolsey said. "I guess this is where you pick up the tale."

Before I told my part, everyone refilled their drink glasses. My headache had eased somewhat, but Ilene insisted I have another of her special concoctions. When everything was settled, I picked up the tale.

"Well, I had reason to believe that the giant metal pumpkin..."

"The Great Pumpkin," Marie suggested, drawing chuckles from around the table with the Charlie Brown reference.

"...was in the Pinery woods. So Marie, Jim and I went to see if we could find it."

"You were obsessed with that pumpkin," Jim complained.

"I'm so glad she was," Cindy told him.

"Anyway, I suggested that we split up..."

"Of course you did," Wolsey said. "Did you not learn anything in Kincardine this summer?"

I glared at him. "I had no reason to believe there was any danger, De-tec-tive," I snapped. "Anyway, I thought I saw something off the trail and went to get a closer look."

"Despite having promised to stay on the trail," Jim pointed out, his voice carrying a tinge of anger.

"Yes, despite that," I stated, embarrassed, before continuing my part of the tale. "Imagine my surprise when it was the giant pumpkin..."

Marie cleared her throat.

"The Great Pumpkin," I corrected, giving her what she wanted. "But it was covered in brush and tree branches as though someone was trying to hide it."

"Imagine that," Wolsey said dryly.

"I only saw the orange because a branch had fallen off and revealed a section. I was going to take a picture of it and then go find Jim and Marie, when Pierre spoke behind me."

"What did he say?"

I frowned. "You know, I'm not sure." I thought for a minute. "I remember recognizing his voice. Then he hit me on the head and I blacked out." I looked at Jim, shocked. "I don't remember what he said!"

Jim patted my hand. "It's the concussion," he told me. "It will come back in time."

"Maybe not," Myrna piped up. She turned to Ilene. "Remember that concussion I got in Vancouver that time? Try as they might, they couldn't get the information they needed, because I just couldn't remember."

Ilene looked at her in shock, clearly surprised that Myrna had mentioned it at all.

I waited a moment, but as no more information was forthcoming, as usual, I decided to continue. "When I woke up, I was tied up and gagged; on the floor of what I realized once my head cleared was the inside of..." I looked over at Marie. "...the Great Pumpkin."

Wolsey groaned. "What did you do next?" he asked.

"He had tied my hands in front of me..."

"Rookie mistake," Myrna supplied, earning her a few more puzzled looks.

"...so I removed the gag and used my teeth to untie the twine around my wrists." I paused. Remembering was actually hard work right now, and it was bringing back my headache. "Then I heard Cindy, and tried to get her free, but there were locks." I looked at her for confirmation and she nodded.

My own eyes teared up this time. "How could someone who supposedly loves another person, do something like that to her?"

The question hung in the air, and no one seemed to have an answer.

"I motioned for her to go for help," Cindy blurted into the silence.

"That's right! I remember that," I said. "I was going to go and then the door opened. It was Pierre. I knew if he got hold of me, he would win. So I just charged at him."

"It was impressive," Cindy said, but after a brief moment she added, "It would have been better if it had worked though."

"I slipped on the boxer shorts..." I began.

"Wait! What boxer shorts?" Wolsey asked incredulously.

"Ah crap. I didn't want to mention that."

"Well you have now," Jim prodded. "So 'fess up."

I sighed. "Fine. He gagged me with a pair of satin boxers in my mouth, covered with duct tape."

Laughter erupted and I winced at the loud sound. The only good part of the pain was that it made them all stop laughing as soon as they noticed.

"Anyway," I continued, eager to get off of the subject of boxer shorts, "I slipped and he went down with me on top of him. He had hold of me and I mouthed off at him."

Marie chuckled. "That's my girl."

"What did you say?" Wolsey asked out of some sort of morbid curiousity.

I smiled. "I told him I'd been called a menace before, and by better men than he."

Wolsey actually barked out a quick laugh.

"He backhanded me and knocked me out again," I continued, after giving the detective an equally quick smile. "I woke up in the back seat of an SUV." I looked at Myrna. "This time with my hands tied behind my back."

"He said we couldn't stay there," Cindy added. "He took Casey to the car first, and then came back for me." She paused, fighting back tears. "He kept the chain attached to the collar, walking with me like I was a dog." She shuddered. "But Casey wasn't there when we got there."

Wolsey nodded sympathetically to Cindy, and then turned to me. "How did you get out of the vehicle?"

"I opened the door and fell out of it," I snapped.

"No, seriously."

I gave him a withering look. "Really? You find that hard to believe?"

"I don't," Marie piped up.

"No one asked you," I retorted.

"Just tell me how you opened the door and escaped," Wolsey growled, swiping his hand over his head.

I sighed. "I told the truth. I put my back to the door and worked at it until I got hold of the door handle. I'm sure if you

224

look, you'll see my blood all over the handle. The stickiness helped me to get a grip on it."

Jim moaned, clearly distressed at this part of the story. I shot him an apologetic look and continued. "The door opened, but I was leaning against it, so..."

Marie laughed, stopping with effort when I glared at her. "So you fell out," she finished for me.

I nodded with a sigh. "Then I ran as fast as I could away. And I ran into you."

"Literally," Jim added, trying to make light of the distressing situation.

I narrowed my eyes at my husband. "Whose side are you on?" I turned to Wolsey. "What were you doing out there anyway?"

Still chuckling at his own joke, Jim looked at Marie. "I guess that's our cue then."

She nodded. "You can take this one, I'll keep taking notes."

Cindy spoke up before we could go any further. "I could really use a break," she announced. "I've been sitting in the same position for ages. I need to stretch my legs."

Wolsey stood up and stretched. "I think we could all use a break," he agreed. "Let's meet back here in an hour."

"Perfect," Ilene said, heading for the front desk. "You are our only guests right now, so I'm going to take it easy and order pizza for everyone. We can finish up over dinner."

Junior looked surprised. "I'm not sure that's a good idea," he protested.

Wolsey shook his head. "Don't worry about it. If anyone gives you a hard time, tell them I overruled you."

We gathered around the huge wooden table in Ilene's kitchen for what was likely the last time. Once we all had some slices of pizza on our plates, none of which contained pumpkin, and drinks before us, we got back down to work.

"Cam, where did we leave off?" Wolsey asked his son the police officer.

I was disappointed that he had not adopted our new nickname for the young man, but you can't win them all. That wasn't going to stop us from using the nickname though.

Junior glanced down at his notes. "Mrs. Robertson had just escaped the vehicle, and ran into you."

I looked at the officer for a sign of a sense of humour, but saw no indication of it. If he was trying to make a joke, he was hiding it well.

"You can call me Casey," I told him. "Mrs. Robertson is my mother-in-law."

"Literally," Jim repeated. "She literally ran into him."

"Can it." I told my husband.

"Yes, my sweet," he chuckled.

Wolsey sighed. "Jim, tell us what happened after the three of you..." He gave me an exasperated look. "...split up."

Jim nodded. "I headed towards Eastwood Drive and Marie went towards the water tower. We were going to enter the woods from the sides and meet up with Casey somewhere in the middle of the wood lot. We both got to the main path at about the same time, but there was no sign of Casey."

"Did you look for her?"

Jim nodded. "Of course we did. We were getting pretty alarmed. But we didn't think she'd been kidnapped. We just thought she might have fallen or something."

"I resemble that remark," I mumbled, my mouth full of Hawaiian pizza.

"And what did you find?" Wolsey asked, ignoring my joke.

Some people just have no sense of humour.

"Nothing, at least not at first," Jim answered Wolsey's question. "But then we had a 'duh' moment and called her cell phone. The weird thing was that we heard it ringing in the direction Marie had just come from."

"From which Marie had come," Marie corrected.

"That's what I said, grammar Nazi," Jim said with a roll of his eyes. "Anyway, when we found Casey's phone relatively far from where she said she'd be, we instantly thought something was wrong."

"Of course," Wolsey agreed.

"And we called you."

"Did you touch the phone?"

"You know we didn't," Jim said, confused.

"I just need you to say so, for the record."

"We didn't touch the phone," Jim stated, looking over at Junior, who wrote the statement down.

Wolsey nodded and everyone quietly ate for a few minutes.

"I could really use a glass of wine," I declared, "so can we get this over with?"

Again, Wolsey nodded, but he was stubbornly silent.

I sighed. "Can someone tell me why you were looking right where I was when I ran into you?"

Wolsey actually chuckled. "We took the cell phone into the station and put a rush on checking it for prints. While we were searching, pretty close to where we...ran into you...the station called to say there were two sets of prints on the phone. Yours and Pierre's."

"You can't get prints done that fast," I scoffed. "That's only on TV."

He shrugged, not bothering to enlighten me on police procedures. "So we were on alert that something we hadn't quite grasped was afoot."

"Afoot?" I scoffed.

"I AM a detective."

I stared at him for a minute, and then shook my head. Maybe he did have a sense of humour. "And the prints belonged to..." I prodded.

"Remember when we processed the scene of Cindy's apartment?" Wolsey asked. "We got Pierre's prints so that we could exclude his prints, since he also lived there."

"And they matched!" Marie exclaimed.

We all processed this information for a moment, and both Junior and I took advantage of the opportunity to take a few bites of pizza. "So I ran into you..." I continued.

"Literally," Jim muttered.

I ignored him this time.

"And it was clear that you had been taken against your will." Upon seeing my blank look, he added, "You were tied up."

I was having trouble remembering details again. I frowned as I concentrated. "Did you shush me?"

"I did. I put you behind me and Jim took you to the ambulance that was waiting at the end of the trail."

"You just picked me up and moved me like I was an errant toddler," I recalled. The detective looked a bit embarrassed, so I continued. "Then what happened?" I asked.

"I think we're done here," Wolsey said instead of answering. I could see he was enjoying himself. "We have all of the information that we need. Officer Wolsey, I will leave you to type up these statements and get the witnesses to sign off on them before they leave town tomorrow."

Junior nodded and gathered up his papers. "Yes sir," he said as he headed out the door.

Wolsey smiled. "Music to a father's ears," he joked.

"Wait!" Marie said as Wolsey made to stand. "You can't just leave us hanging! What happened after Casey was out of the way?"

He laughed and sat back down. "Alright," he said. "I had a definite direction in which to go, and I drew my sidearm. When I rounded the bend I saw a dark SUV with the back driver's side door open. On the other side of the vehicle were Pierre and Cindy." He turned a sympathetic look on the young woman. "She was clearly not there of her own free will."

Cindy took over. "Pierre tried to run!"

"What a coward," Helen spat.

Cindy nodded. "He just dropped the chains and ran back the way we came." She looked at Wolsey. "The detective motioned for some other officers to go after him, and he came to help me."

"I wasn't getting through those locks, and I wasn't willing to wait for Pierre to give me the keys," Wolsey said, "so I cut through the leather with my knife."

"It felt so good to get that thing off of me! And it felt even better when they led Pierre past us in handcuffs," Cindy admitted. "Does that make me a bad person?"

"Pierre is the bad person dear," Myrna told her. We all muttered in agreement.

"You should have spit in his face," Lori said.

"Or kicked him between the legs," Velma suggested.

"You should have decked him," Helen added.

"Now ladies," Wolsey admonished. "All of those things are classified as assault." He rose to his feet. "Do you have everything you need?" he asked Marie.

She nodded. "I have your number if I think of anything else."

I gasped. "My phone!"

Wolsey smiled, his eyes twinkling. "Junior will give it back to you tomorrow."

My mouth dropped open in shock at his use of our nickname for his son.

"He's not going to be happy if that name sticks, by the way," he added on his way out the door.

The evening ended shortly after his departure. Cindy and her friends headed out for what looked like would be an evening of drinking, friendship, and tears at one of the girls' apartments.

After the rest of us made plans to meet up for one last breakfast before we went our separate ways, Myrna and Ilene insisted on cleaning up after the dinner. For his part, Andrew seemed content to supervise their activity. Marie made a quick exit to go home, her evening ahead about to be taken up by writing up the entire sordid tale for the next day's newspaper.

As for us, we headed upstairs to our turret room for our last night in town. It may have taken me a little extra time to get back up the stairs, but I'll never admit that in public. Jim drew me a hot bath, but instead of that glass of wine I'd mentioned earlier, he brought me a pumpkin spice tea. After a long, hot, muscle easing soak, I joined Jim in the main room, planting a big kiss of gratitude on his lips. We sat in the chairs looking out over the lake and enjoyed the peace and quiet.

I would have had a good sleep that night if Jim hadn't kept waking me up every hour or so to make sure that I was still alive. I couldn't be too angry with him though, I realized. Once again, without even trying, I had frightened him. But after the fourth time of being wakened from a deep sleep, I finally had to be firm in telling him to allow me to get some sleep.

A girl can only take so much pampering, after all.

THE TRAVELLING KLUTZ

The one thing about visiting a place that you come to love is that you can always return. And the one thing about meeting people who become friends or even family is that you can keep in touch.

That doesn't mean that saying farewell, until we meet again, isn't difficult. It is. But you can do so in the knowledge that you will return someday. Or perhaps reunite in a new place, where you can enjoy new experiences and build more memories.

All you have to do is open yourself up to the uniqueness of the places and the people you visit. Because it is true what they say - travel is one of the few things that make you richer.

Chapter 21

Things were much quieter when we descended the stairs of The Mariner's Rest for the final time. Pumpkinfest was over, so the inn had no guests other than the two of us, and Myrna and Andrew.

We settled in at one of the larger tables in the Port in a Storm Cafe and were soon joined by Ilene, bearing coffee.

"That's just coffee, right?" Jim asked.

Ilene asked. "Absolutely. The pumpkin flavouring has been put to rest for another year."

"And not a moment too soon," he stated, turning over the mug at his place setting enthusiastically.

"It's so quiet," I stated the obvious.

She nodded. "We're entering the quiet time now," she said. "There will be a bit of a spike over Thanksgiving, but we close over Christmas, and things are much quieter over the winter." She looked appraisingly at me. "Do you need another special tea?"

I shook my head. "The pain killers the paramedics gave me seem to be working," I told her, "as long as I don't do anything wild and crazy."

Myrna and Andrew entered the cafe and came over to join us.

"It's quiet," Andrew said by way of greeting.

Ilene just shrugged. "Bacon, eggs, hash browns and toast all around?" she asked.

We all murmured agreement and she sat down and joined us. Before we could express our surprise, a member of her kitchen staff came out with a couple more carafes of coffee and took away the now empty one.

"Breakfast will be out shortly," the woman said before returning to the kitchen.

"I'm so glad you can join us and relax," I told Ilene warmly.

She smiled. "So am I. I feel like I miss all of the excitement sometimes."

Myrna snorted. "I think we've had plenty of excitement over the years."

We looked from one to the other, but neither of the women seemed about to expand on Myrna's statement. Before I could question them any further, Wolsey came into the cafe and sank down into a chair at our table with a sigh.

"Off duty Detective?" Andrew asked.

He nodded in response as he poured himself a coffee.

"Well Ed," Jim said, using the detective's first name since he was no longer on the clock. "Never a dull moment, eh?"

Wolsey looked at him and laughed. "Not when this one is around," he answered, nodding in my direction. "Where is your number three, anyway?"

"Marie had a late night," I answered. "We're going to drop by and say goodbye to her on our way home."

"Have you decided where we're going next?" Myrna asked me.

I looked at her in surprise. "We?"

She shrugged. "I'm enjoying these little jaunts," she told me. She looked over at Ilene. "They remind me of old times." Turning back to me and added, "It's quite entertaining waiting to see what kind of trouble you are going to get into."

Jim laughed, but at my annoyed look he quickly sobered.

"I don't ALWAYS get into trouble, you know."

"You're two for two," Ed observed dryly.

"So Ed," Jim changed the subject. "Everything squared away with the case?"

The detective nodded. "Actually, I have your statements here to sign," he said, digging into his briefcase and producing a file folder. "Once you sign these, the crown attorney will have all he needs to prosecute."

I took the file with my name on it and the pen he offered. "Pierre won't be getting out on bail, will he? I worry about Cindy if he does."

He watched me sign the document. "I doubt it, considering we caught him in the act. He's charged with two counts of kidnapping and forcible confinement, assault and assault with a weapon, obstruction of a police investigation, and possession of stolen property."

236

"That's a lot of charges," Andrew observed. "What exactly was stolen?"

"And I don't understand the obstruction charges," I added.

Ed nodded, handing Jim his folder. Looking mischievously at me, he answered Jim's question first. "The owner of the Great Pumpkin says it went missing about a year ago. He just never reported it. And the obstruction charges stem from all of the items he scattered around town to make us think Cindy was just laying low."

I nodded in understanding. "He planted the cell phone, the jacket and bracelet for someone to find." I considered that for a moment before adding, "What are the odds that it would be me finding them all?"

Wolsey snorted, but otherwise ignored my comment. "Anyway," he continued, "if Pierre does get bail, I sincerely doubt he'll be able to pay the bond. And if he somehow manages to do so, there will be conditions and a restraining order against him. The police here will keep a close eye on him and Cindy."

"Are we going to have to come back and testify?" Jim asked with trepidation as he signed his statement. "Because that is getting tedious."

"Only if he pleads not guilty," Ed answered with a chuckle. He gathered the two folders and put them aside. "I'll drop these off to the station before I head out."

We were silent for a while as the breakfast food arrived. Two waitresses placed it in the centre of the table family style and we all helped ourselves to the platters of scrambled eggs, bacon, sausages, hash browns, and white and brown toast with various local jams, marmalades and honey. Pitchers of orange juice, and a bottle of champagne for those who wanted mimosas, followed and, after filling our fluted glasses, we held them up for a toast.

"To friends," I said.

"And adventure," Myrna added.

"So, where ARE you off to next?" Ed asked. "I want to know where to avoid if at all possible."

"Funny, De-tec-tive," I drawled. "I'm not doing any more travelling for the magazine until spring, actually."

"She needs time to heal," Jim half joked.

"You know Casey, you might want to try Yoga or stretching," Ilene advised. "You'll snap back a lot faster from injury, or even avoid getting hurt at all. It would improve your balance and agility."

I sighed. "That might be a good idea," I conceded. "This getting hurt thing is really getting old and I'm tired of it."

"You're not the only one, my sweet," Jim agreed, patting my hand and then quickly pulling his hand back at my wince.

I turned to our hostess. "I've been meaning to tell you Ilene, that I really love the paintings on the walls of the inn. Are they really yours?"

Ilene beamed with pride. "Yes they are."

"Is there any chance I can get my hands on one with a local scene?" I asked. "All of our artwork at home features places we've been and I'd love to add one of your watercolours to the collection."

"I'm sure we can arrange something," she said happily. "I will e-mail you pictures of what I have available."

"That would be wonderful, thank you!"

There was another lull in conversation again as we ate.

"So, we're looking at spring then?" Myrna asked, not giving up on getting a destination out of me. She was definitely like a dog with a bone at the moment.

I sighed. "Definitely not before then," I told her, filling my mouth with crispy bacon with an appreciative sigh, buying myself a few minutes of peace. Or so I thought.

"And where will we be going?" Ilene asked. Jim and I both looked at her in shock.

"You're coming too?" I exclaimed. "I wouldn't think you could get away from The Mariner's Rest."

She shrugged. "I have a good staff," she told me. "I can't let Myrna relive our glory days without me after all. And if I can plan ahead..." She left the thought dangling and everyone looked at me in anticipation.

I sighed and relented, even though I wasn't entirely certain of where my next article would take me. "I'm thinking of going up to Tobermory. They have the national park up there, the Grotto, and Flowerpot Island, and the shipwrecks where people dive and snorkel." I paused, taking an appreciative drink of my mimosa.

"The Bruce Peninsula and Tobermory would be an excellent choice," Ilene agreed.

"But you have another possibility?" Myrna pressed.

I frowned at her. "You just won't give up, will you?" I teased. "I was also thinking of possibly writing about Goderich," I continued. "They've come so far since that tornado in 2011; they deserve to be in the spotlight for something good. They're in another county, and it might be time to switch it up and go somewhere other than the Bruce, which I used for the first two articles. And Goderich has a double sunset, the downtown square that's really a roundabout, and the reportedly haunted historic jail."

"Oh, I haven't been to Goderich in ages," Myrna enthused. "I always seem to go north, because Ilene is here."

"Goderich would be fun," Ilene agreed. "Remember that time when we danced at that reception for the Governor-General..."

Myrna quickly interrupted her. "They don't want to hear about that," she insisted.

"Actually, I'd love to."

The two women ignored me and engaged in a stare down. Andrew took pity on me. "Perhaps when next we get together," he suggested.

I sighed at yet another opportunity to learn more about the two enigmatic and mysterious women slipped through my fingers. "Anyway, I'll have to see what my editor thinks."

"Let us know," Ed more demanded than requested.

"Ooh, both of those would be great," Andrew declared.

"I certainly hope so," I said, memories of the last few days still foremost in my mind.

Jim put his arm around me gently. "Anywhere is fine, as long as we are together," he declared.

We all held up our glasses one more time, to a rousing chorus of "Cheers."

The End

Please help an author out and leave a review of this book at Amazon and/or Goodreads. Your help getting the word out is greatly appreciated.

Pumpkin Recipes

Did the pumpkin goodies in this book sound delicious to you? All of them were sourced from family and friends, who were kind enough to provide their favourite pumpkin recipes for me to share with my readers. My niece even created a recipe just for us!

The recipes are listed in order of suitability for breakfast to dinner. Enjoy.

Pumpkin Spice Latte

Courtesy of Kathy Ashton, Beta Sigma Phi sister, Chatham ON
Ingredients

- 2 cups milk
- 2 tablespoons canned pumpkin puree
- 1 tablespoon maple syrup, or more to taste
- 1 tablespoon vanilla
- ¼ teaspoon cinnamon
- 1/8 teaspoon ground ginger
- 1/16 teaspoon ground nutmeg
- Dash ground cloves
- ½ cup strong black coffee or espresso

Directions

1. Wisk together all ingredients except for the coffee.

2. Heat the mixture on the stove or in the microwave until very hot, but not boiling.
3. Add the coffee and whisk, or use a frother, or blend and whirl until frothy.
4. Top with whipped cream and a sprinkle of ground cinnamon.
5. Enjoy!

Pumpkin Porridge and Oats with protein

Courtesy of John Culbert Jr., nephew, Muskoka, ON
Ingredients

- 2/3 cup of Rogers' "Porridge and Oats Mix"
- 1 scoop of protein powder (optional)
- 1/4 cup of a pure pumpkin (NOT pie filling)
- A few dashes of pumpkin pie spice
- One squirt of maple syrup to sweeten.
- Unsweetened almond milk to make it a batter-like consistency

Directions

1. Combine all of the ingredients.
2. Leave in the fridge overnight.
3. Stir in the morning
4. Add a dollop of Cool-Whip if desired.

Pumpkin Muffins

Courtesy of Ilene Scott, Beta Sigma Phi sister, Port Elgin, ON

Ingredients
- 4 eggs
- 1 ½ cups vegetable oil
- 3 cups all purpose flour
- 2 tsp baking soda
- 1 tsp salt

- ¼ tsp nutmeg
- 2 cups raisins
- 1 ½ cups white sugar
- 14 oz can pumpkin
- 1 tsp cinnamon
- 2 tsp baking powder
- ¼ tsp ground cloves
- ½ tsp ginger

Directions

1. Preheat oven to 350 F
2. Beat eggs. Add sugar, pumpkin and oil, mix well.
3. Add flour, spices and raisins. Mix.
4. Bake 15 - 20 minutes.

Pumpkin French toast with Brown Sugar Cinnamon Butter
Courtesy of Karen McIsaac, sister, Orillia, ON

Ingredients

- 10 slices Brioche bread
  For the dip:
- 6 oz pumpkin, canned
- 3 Eggs
- 2 tbsp Flour
- 2 tsp Vanilla
- 3/4 cup Milk
  For the butter:
- 4 tbsp Butter, softened
- 1 1/3 tbsp Brown sugar

- 1 tsp Cinnamon
- 1/4 tsp Nutmeg

Directions for butter

1. Combine the butter, cinnamon, brown sugar, and nutmeg in a small bowl and whisk until mixed well.
2. Preheat a pan at medium high heat, and coat with cooking spray or butter.

Directions for dip

1. Mix eggs, milk, vanilla, and pumpkin. Whisk well.
2. In separate bowl, mix flour, cinnamon, and brown sugar.
3. Add dry ingredients into wet and whisk until combined.

Directions for toast

1. Dip bread into egg mixture, coating both sides. Shake off excess.
2. Add to hot pan and cook until golden brown, about 3-4 minutes per side.
3. Top with butter pieces.

Pumpkin Loaf

Courtesy of Alice Scott, mother-in-law of Beta Sigma Phi sister, Port Elgin, ON

Ingredients

- 1 2/3 cup flour
- 1 teaspoon baking soda
- ¼ teaspoon each of cinnamon, baking powder, salt and nutmeg
- 1/3 cup shortening
- ¼ teaspoon vanilla

- 1 1/3 cup sugar
- 2 eggs
- 1 cup pumpkin
- 1/3 cup water
- ½ cup pecans

Directions

1. Preheat oven at 350 F
2. Sift together flour, soda, cinnamon, baking powder, salt and nutmeg, set aside
3. Cream together shortening, vanilla and sugar
4. Mix together pumpkin and water, beat in eggs one at a time
5. Stir dry and creamed mixtures alternately into flour mixture. Mix well.
6. Add pecans
7. Pour into greased or lined loaf pan
8. Bake 60 minutes.

Pumpkin Soup

Courtesy of Ilene Scott, Beta Sigma Phi sister, Port Elgin, ON

Ingredients

- ¼ cup butter
- 14 oz can pumpkin
- 2 cups vegetable stock
- ½ tsp. sugar
- 1/8 - ¼ teaspoon nutmeg

- 1 cup half and half cream
- Salt and pepper to taste
- ½ large onion, sliced
- 2 cups chicken stock
- 1 Bay leaf
- ¼ - ½ teaspoon curry powder
- ¼ cup chopped parsley
- 1 cup apple sauce
- Sour cream and paprika (optional)

Directions

1. In large saucepan, melt butter over medium heat, and sauté onions
2. Stir in pumpkin, stock, bay leaf, sugar, curry, nutmeg and parsley.
3. Bring to a boil
4. Reduce heat and simmer, uncovered, for 15 minutes, stirring occasionally.
5. Puree in food processor or blender.
6. Return to low heat. Add cream, apple sauce, salt and pepper.
7. Simmer for 5 to 10 minutes
8. Garnish with sour cream and paprika and serve hot.

Zesty Pumpkin Soup

Courtesy of Ilene Scott, Beta Sigma Phi sister, Port Elgin, ON

Ingredients

- ¼ cup butter
- 1 cup chopped onion
- 1 garlic clove, crushed
- 1 teaspoon curry powder
- ¼ teaspoon ground Coriander, or to taste
- Sour cream and Chives (optional)
- 3 cups chicken broth
- 1 ¾ cups (16 oz) can pumpkin
- 1 cup half & half cream
- ½ teaspoon salt
- 1/8 teaspoon crushed red pepper

Directions

1. In large saucepan, melt butter and sauté onion and garlic until soft.
2. Add curry powder, salt, coriander and red pepper, and cook for one minute.
3. Add broth and boil gently, uncovered, for up to 20 minutes
4. Stir in pumpkin and half & half cream. Cook for five minutes
5. Pour into blender and blend until creamy.
6. Return to low heat.
7. Garnish with a dollop of sour cream and chopped chives, if desired.

Pumpkin Spice Pretzels

Courtesy of Emma Hammond of <u>Babybakes</u>, niece, Orillia, ON, devised specifically for use in this book

Ingredients

- 1 cup of milk
- 2-1/4 teaspoon quick rising yeast
- 3 tbsp brown sugar
- 2 tbsp soft butter
- 2-1/4 cups all purpose flour
- 1 teaspoon salt
- 1/3 cup baking soda
- 1 tablespoon cinnamon sugar
- 1/4 cup icing sugar
- 1/2 tsp pumpkin pie spice
- 1 teaspoon of vanilla
- 1 teaspoon water

Directions

1. Heat milk in saucepan over medium heat until steaming.
2. Transfer to mixing bowl, sprinkle yeast on top. Wait 2 to 3 minutes until the yeast is soft.
3. Stir in brown sugar.
4. Transfer to kitchen aid bowl, and with a wooden spoon mix in butter and 1 cup flour until mixture makes a gooey like paste.

5. Add remaining 1-1/4 cup flour and salt, and set on low/medium speed with dough hook until a tacky dough forms.
6. Place the ball of dough in a greased bowl and spray top of dough with cooking spray. Cover with plastic wrap and let rise for 1 hour.
7. Preheat oven to 450 degrees Fahrenheit.
8. Cut dough into 5 equal parts and roll with palms of hand, starting in the middle and rolling outwards, slapping dough to lengthen.
9. Roll into pretzel shape.
10. Add baking soda to 4 cups warm water.
11. Dunk pretzels into water solution quickly and place them on baking sheet. Sprinkle with cinnamon sugar.
12. Bake 14 minutes, rotating pans halfway through.
13. While baking, mix icing sugar, vanilla, water, and pumpkin pie spice together to make glaze.
14. When pretzels come out, move to cooking wrack and brush with glaze.
15. Eat!

Makes 5 pretzels

Pumpkin Bread

Courtesy of Donna Keech, Beta Sigma Phi sister, Chatham, Ontario

Ingredients
- 3 ½ cups flour
- 3 cups sugar

- ½ teaspoon baking powder
- 1 ½ teaspoons salt
- 1 teaspoon each of cloves, nutmeg, and cinnamon
- 1 cup oil
- 4 eggs
- 2 cups canned pumpkin
- ¾ cups chopped nuts of choice
- ¾ cup water

Directions

1. Preheat oven to 325 degrees Fahrenheit.
2. Sift first seven ingredients together into large bowl, making a well in the centre.
3. Add remaining ingredients and beat with mixer until blended.
4. Pour batter into three 9 x 5 x 3" loaf pans.
5. Bake 1 ½ hours.

Spicy Pumpkin Hummus

Courtesy of Kathy Ashton, Beta Sigma Phi sister, Chatham ON

Ingredients

- ¼ cup tahini
- ¼ cup lemon juice
- ½ clove big garlic

- 2 teaspoons olive oil
- ½ - 1 teaspoon salt
- 1 teaspoon cumin
- ¼ teaspoon cayenne
- ½ cup canned, unsweetened pumpkin puree
- 1 425 g can chick peas, drained and rinsed, skins in tact

Directions

1. Mix tahini and lemon juice in food processor for at least 1 minute.
2. Add garlic, olive oil, salt, cumin, cayenne and pumpkin puree to food processor and mix for another minute.
3. Add half of chick peas, process for 1 minute.
4. Add second half of chick peas and process for up to 2 minutes.
5. Add 2-3 tablespoons water, if desired, to adjust consistency.
6. Sprinkle with paprika and or several pumpkin seeds.
7. Serve with crackers or flatbreads.

Pumpkin Crunch Cake

Courtesy of Donna Keech, Beta Sigma Phi sister, Chatham ON

Ingredients

- 1 package golden cake mix
- 796 ml can pure pumpkin
- 370 ml can evaporated milk
- 3 eggs
- 1 cup sugar

- 4 teaspoons Pumpkin pie spice
- ½ teaspoon salt
- 1 cup chopped pecans (optional)
- Whipped topping or ice cream

Directions

1. Preheat oven to 350 degrees Fahrenheit.
2. Grease 13" x 9" pan.
3. Combine pumpkin, milk, eggs, sugar, spices and salt in a large bowl.
4. Pour into pan.
5. Sprinkle with dry cake mix evenly over pumpkin mixture.
6. Top with pecans.
7. Drizzle with melted butter.
8. Bake for 50 to 55 minutes until golden brown.
9. Cool and serve with whipped cream or ice cream.
10. Refrigerate leftovers.

Pumpkin-Coconut Cheesecake

Courtesy of Lynne Stephenson, Beta Sigma Phi sister, Chatham, ON

Ingredients

- 2 cups graham cracker crumbs
- 1 ½ cups toasted desiccated or flaked coconut
- ¼ cup granulated sugar
- ½ cup unsalted butter, melted
- 4 eggs
- 1 cup canned pumpkin puree; no spices added

- ½ cup packed brown sugar
- 1 teaspoon cinnamon
- ½ tsp each ground nutmeg, ginger and salt
- 2 - 8 oz package regular cream cheese at room temperature
- ½ cup granulated sugar
- ½ cup whipping cream
- 1 teaspoon vanilla

Directions

1. For crust, preheat oven to 350 F. Lightly butter sides and bottom of 10" spring form pan. In a bowl, stir crumbs with 1 cup toasted coconut, ¼ cup granulated sugar and butter until evenly moist. Press over bottom and partway up sides of prepared pan. Bake in centre of oven until edges are golden, about 10 minutes. Cool on rack. Keep oven on.
2. Meanwhile, for filling, whisk eggs in large bowl. Whisk in pumpkin, brown sugar and seasonings. Cut cheese into cubes and place in large bowl. Using an electric mixer, beat in granulated sugar, and then beat in cream, vanilla and pumpkin mixture, scraping down side of bowl if needed, until well mixed. Pour over warm crust.
3. Bake in centre of a 325 F oven until filling is almost set when pan is jiggled, 55 to 60 minutes. Place pan on rack to cool. Immediately run a knife around inside pan edge to loosen crust and prevent cracking. When cooled to room temperature, refrigerate until cold, at least 4 hours. Remove from pan. Sprinkle with remaining coconut.

Prep time: 20 minutes Baking time: 1 hour 5 minutes Standing time: 40 minutes

Makes 10-12 wedges

Pumpkin Crumble

Courtesy of Ilene Scott, Beta Sigma Phi sister, Port Elgin

Ingredients
- 3 eggs
- 1 large can pumpkin puree
- 1 teaspoon ground cloves
- 1 28 oz can Carnation Milk
- 1 teaspoon Cinnamon
- 1 cup white sugar
- 1 Golden or white cake mix
- ½ pound butter, melted
- Slivered almonds to taste

Directions
1. Preheat oven to 350 degrees Fahrenheit.
2. Mix first six ingredients and pour into a greased 9 x 13 " pan.
3. Sprinkle cake mix evenly over mixture.
4. Pour melted butter over cake mix.
5. Sprinkle with slivered almonds.
6. Bake for one hour or until browned on top.

Orange pumpkin cake

Courtesy of Toyce Smith, Beta Sigma Phi sister, Chatham, ON

Ingredients
- 3/4   Cup shortening
- 2 1/4   Cup packed brown sugar
- 3   Eggs
- 1 1/2   Cups canned pumpkin
- 1 1/2   Teaspoons baking powder
- 1 1/2   Teaspoons ground cinnamon
- 3/4   Teaspoons baking soda
- 3/4   Teaspoon ground nutmeg
- 1/2   Cup thawed orange juice concentrate
- 3/4   Teaspoon ground allspice
- 2 1/2   Cups all-purpose flour
- 1/3   Cup 2% milk

FILLING:

- Package (8 ounces) cream cheese, softened
- Cup confectioners' sugar
- 1/2   Teaspoon pumpkin pie spice
- Carton (8 ounces) frozen whipped topping, thawed
- 1/2   Cup canned pumpkin
- 1/4   Cup caramel ice cream topping (I have used Eagle Brand Dulce de Leche topping)
- 1/4   Cup coarsely chopped pecans

Directions
1. Preheat oven to 350F.
2. In a large bowl, cream shortening and brown sugar until light and fluffy.   Add eggs, one at a time, beating well after each addition.   Stir in pumpkin and orange juice concentrate.   Combine the flour, baking powder,

cinnamon, baking soda, nutmeg and allspice; add to the creamed mixture alternately with milk, beating well after each addition.

3. Pour into two greased and floured 9 inch round baking pans. Bake at 350F for 28-32 minutes or until a toothpick inserted in the center comes out clean. Cool for 10 minutes before removing from pans to wire racks to cool completely.

4. For filling, in a large bowl, beat cream cheese until light and fluffy. Add confectioners' sugar and pie spice; beat until smooth. Fold in whipped topping and pumpkin.

5. Cut each cake horizontally into two layers. Place bottom layer on a serving plate; spread with a fourth of the filling. Repeat layers three times. Sprinkle with pecans; drizzle with caramel topping. Store in the refrigerator.

Sensational Double Layer Pumpkin Pie

Courtesy of Ilene Scott, Beta Sigma Phi sister, Port Elgin, Ontario

Ingredients
- 1 package Philadelphia Cream Cheese, softened
- 1 cup plus 1 tablespoon half & half cream or milk
- 1 tablespoon sugar
- 1 ½ cups Cool Whip, thawed
- 1 Graham Cracker Pie Crust (6 oz)
- 2 packages Jello Vanilla Instant Pudding
- 1 can pumpkin (16 oz)

- 1 teaspoon cinnamon
- ¼ teaspoon ginger
- ¼ teaspoon ground cloves

Directions

1. Mix cream cheese, 1 tablespoon half & half and sugar with wire whisk until smooth.
2. Gently stir in whipped topping.
3. Spread on bottom of crust.
4. Pour 1 cup half & half into mixing bowl.
5. Add pudding mixes and beat with whisk until well blended, up to two minutes.
6. Let stand three minutes.
7. Stir in pumpkin and spices, mix well.
8. Spread over cream cheese layer.
9. Refrigerate at least 2 hours.
10. Garnish with additional whipped topping and nuts as desired.

Chocolate Pumpkin Cupcakes

And because I LOVE cupcakes and must have them here, this is one from me.

Ingredients

- 1 Fudge Marble Cake Mix
- 3 eggs
- 1/3 cup oil
- 1 cup milk
- 2 tablespoon milk

- 1/2 cup canned pumpkin purée
- 1/2 teaspoon cinnamon
- Smarties or M & M's
- 1 jar of Marshmallow Fluff or Crème

Directions

1. Preheat oven to 350oF. Line 2 muffin trays with paper liners.
2. Whisk main cake mix, eggs, and 1 cup milk in a large mixing bowl until well combined.
3. Transfer 1 ½ cups of the batter to another mixing bowl.
4. To it, add in the 2 tbsp of milk and the cocoa packet from the cake mix.
5. Stir until well combined and there are no more lumps of cocoa.
6. To the remaining batter in the large mixing bowl, add the pumpkin, cinnamon. Stir until well combined.
7. Fill each liner 3/4 full. Use cocoa batter on the bottom and top it with the pumpkin batter.
8. Bake 20-25 min, rotating halfway, until a toothpick inserted into the centre of the cupcakes come out clean.
9. Remove from the oven; let cool 10 min before removing cupcakes to cool completely on a wire rack.
10. Top cupcakes with some Marshmallow Fluff and broil for 5 min for a similar effect.
11. Add Smarties or M & M eyes on side of cupcake top. Eat the left over candy.

Pumpkin Dog Treats

Courtesy of Bonney Green, Beta Sigma Phi sister, Chatham, Ontario

These might have kept the dog walker's unruly pack under control.

- 2 cups spelt flour (or whole wheat)
- 3 tbsp ground flaxseed
- 1 tsp cinnamon
- 1 tsp ginger
- 1/2 cup protein of choice (see note below)
- 2/3 cup plain canned pumpkin
- 2 eggs
- 1/4 cup pure maple syrup *

Directions

1. Preheat oven to 300F.
2. Combine dry ingredients.
3. Whisk protein, pumpkin, eggs and maple syrup until smooth, then add to dry ingredients. Mix well.
4. Treats can be rolled out and cut with a bone-shaped cutter in an appropriate size for your dog.
5. Bake for about 30 minutes.
6. Cool completely, then store in an airtight container or resealable bag on the fridge or freezer.

If you're less ambitious, they work just as well as small drop cookies. My Miss Sophie says they taste just as good that way and they're ready to eat sooner. I use a scant teaspoon of batter for hers because she's a little terrier and needs to watch her girlish figure.

Note: For protein you can use peanut butter, or lightly cooked meat pureed with a bit of broth. Sophie is very happy when I use pureed beef or chicken liver, but any left-over meat works too.

 * Do not use table syrup. Some brands may contain artificial sweeteners that could be toxic for your dog.

I loved how intriguing it was. It kept me interested and I couldn't put it down. I also loved how detailed the places were, which made me want to visit myself. ~ Amazon reviewer

I almost passed on getting this book. I am glad now that I got it AND that it didn't get lost among my many other books to read. I have spent an enjoyable few days reading it. The travel information between the chapters is clever and creative. I appreciate it being well edited. Great characters. ~ Goodreads reviewer

As lifelong Kincardine/Bruce Beach Cottagers, *The Piper Sniper*...has a special place in our hearts! ~ Reader message

Very enjoyable book! I really enjoyed this book. It moved along at a good pace and I couldn't put it down. I had to find out who did it and what was going to happen next. The interaction with the characters is very well done. I look forward to reading more of this series. ~ book enthusiast

A must-read for an adventurous trip!! ~ Angie

THE TRAVELLING KLUTZ

Praise for *Urgent Quest at Pumpkinfest*
Do you like hilariously funny cozy mysteries? This book is for you!!
I didn't think Ms. Young could top the comedy from the first
novel, but no, was I mistaken!! I had tears running down my face I
was laughing so hard at times!!

The mystery is a good one, many characters I loved from the first
novel returned along with some interesting new ones, and Ms.
Young's intricate knowledge of the small Ontario town of Port
Elgin is wonderful. ~ Amazon reviewer

Great Book. I loved the book. I enjoy reading the mishaps of Casey
and I always want to know what is going to happen next. ~
Amazon reviewer

I can't remember when I have laughed so hard while reading a
book! (Unless it was while reading the first book in this series!)

Truly hilarious! ... I am really enjoying all the characters...and I can hardly wait for their next adventure! ~ Goodreads reviewer

A gem of a book. I just found this author and I really enjoy the klutzy travel writer. I hope she will write more with these characters. ~ book enthusiast

THE TRAVELLING KLUTZ

Praise for *Christmas Tree Mystery*
Another wonderfully hilarious instalment in the Travel Writer cozy mystery series! ... Highly recommend! ~ Goodreads reviewer

Wow! Television sci-fi and mystery fans will enjoy! I really like this author's set of characters and then, in this book, she throws in so many sci-fi references (Star Trek, Firefly, etc.) that mystery lovers or sci-fi lovers will enjoy this. ~ book enthusiast

Another hilarious adventure for poor Casey and the gang. Angie

THE TRAVELLING KLUTZ

sceneries. The reader was then led into the mystery part very casually, and then surprised out of nowhere. I must admit that I did not guess who it was until the very last pages; in fact, I had chosen several others who I thought would have "done the deed". Good job, Kelly. You write interesting books. Keep up the good work! ~ Reader e-mail

Loved this book ... Armchair travelling and a mystery. I am going to read the others in the series... Anita, Goodreads

Following Casey through this series, you laugh a little, cry a little, and a lot of sitting on the edge waiting to see what's next for her husband and friends. Love it. Angie

Praise for *A Ghost Named Joe*
I just wanted to tell you that I... read your book "A Ghost Named Joe". Your book is so life like and a very good read. I could imagine Joe coming back to find something in the house and I could actually see him looking for something. You are a very talented writer. ~ Reader message

Praise for *Say It Isn't So, Joe*

I really enjoyed this book. I love the way she mixes humour and mystery and I found it to be a very good read for gloomy days or any day but it did brighten those greys, gloomy ones for me ~Sandra, Goodreads reviewer

This is a new and charming paranormal murder mystery from author Kelly Young. It has a very interesting premise, in which the protagonist can see and hear ghosts, who then help her solve the mystery. There are other characters (including the ghosts) who add to the plotline.
Highly recommend! – Deb, Goodreads reviewer

This is an incredible author and (I'm) proud to own 4 of her books...She has a way of drawing you into her books and you simply can not help but loving her characters. A joy to read! ~ Reader message.

Love to read any of Kelly's books. Adventurous and learn something new about something or someplace every time. Keep on putting those thoughts in print. ~ Reader message.

Excellent book, very well written! An intriguing mystery. ~ Barbara Godin, author

Praise for *Kisses in the Moonlight Volume 2: Tales from the Other Side*

Finished this book yesterday, just loved it. Revenge was sweet in "Kisses in the Moonlight – A Tale from the Other Side"! "A Ghost Named Joe" was humorous and yet very touching – especially the protectiveness of Magic. "Eaten Alive" had a bit of jolt to it after Natasha moves away and finds another "friend/victim" to cast her deadly "spell" onto. WOW, didn't see that coming! In "A Touch of Knowledge" it was an excellent example of how greed can overcome a person and ultimately be their demise – it was one of those stories you had to keep on reading to see how far Katya would take her greed (addiction) before it overtook her sensibility. I loved "The Plant Killer" – let me tell you, it will be a long time before I buy another plant and have it die on me. Especially the viney ones and the snake plant. Loved it when that message popped up after they found her body "FLORA OUT" – great ending for the story and the book. Now that one was spooky!

Ghosts, zombies and killers galore in this second creepy compilation of paranormal short stories! Highly recommend! ~ Goodreads/Amazon review

I absolutely loved this book. Kelly is a fantastic author and she has yet to disappoint me... I have found that once I start reading, I finish the story because I simply have to know how it ends...These stories grab you and lure you in to an entirely new world of suspenseful reading. ~ J.M.

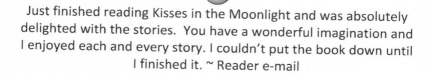

Just finished reading Kisses in the Moonlight and was absolutely delighted with the stories. You have a wonderful imagination and I enjoyed each and every story. I couldn't put the book down until I finished it. ~ Reader e-mail

Praise for *The Six Thousand*

Loved this book so much!This is a futuristic book we all wish would actually happen! Very well written and thought-provoking storyline! Highly recommend! ~ Amazon reviewer

Enjoyed this book immensely. I thought this was a superbly written book and once I started it, I had to read all the way to the end. No starting and stopping this story for sure. A very timely story and would be a great choice for a book club as the variety of themes brought up within the story lend to discussion. ~ Amazon reviewer

It's a great read, and I enjoyed it very much. I could see the parallel to the evils of today's world, and would not be opposed to seeing this happen, because there are so many good people in the world that deserve better. Well done and highly recommend! ~ Goodreads/Amazon reviewer

This book was so good and kept my interest throughout. I enjoyed learning more about the Legion and seeing different relationships and friendships build through the story. ~Goodreads reviewer

Quite the page-turner! A creative and thought-provoking storyline that is well constructed and leaves the reader wanting more. Written in such a way one really feels connected to each character and can imagine the world created from a single idea. Would read again! Samantha, Goodreads

Praise for *Flurries Ending*

Just finished *Flurries Ending*. Enjoyed it immensely...Your lead character Kim drove me crazy with her lists. I know so many people like her. So true of some people. You kept her solid with her traits till the end. ~ Reader e-mail

Praise for *The Mitten Tree*

A Treasure! This is a wonderful story about leading a child to want to help others. It also demonstrates the huge generosity of knitters and crocheters. It gives a girl a reason to want to learn to knit. Although not a picture book, the pictures that are included display nicely on my monochrome Kindle. ~ Donna

Also by this author

The Travel Writer Cozy Mystery Series
The Piper Sniper: A Travel Writer Cozy Mystery #1

Urgent Quest at Pumpkinfest: A Travel Writer Cozy Mystery #2

Christmas Tree Mystery: A Travel Writer Cozy Mystery #3

Lethal Shot on Flowerpot: A Travel Writer Cozy Mystery #4

The Travel Writer Day Trips Cozy Mystery series

Wine and Whines: A Travel Writer Day Trips Cozy Mysteries #1

The Haunted and Harassed Paranormal Mystery series

A Ghost Named Joe: A Haunted and Harassed Paranormal Mystery #0.5

Say it Isn't So, Joe: A Haunted and Harassed Paranormal Mystery #1

Speculative Fiction
Trumping the States

Putin' it to the States: A Trumping the States sequel

Short Stories
Kisses in the Moonlight And Other Short Tales: Volume 1

Kisses in the Moonlight and Other Short Tales: Volume 2

Stand Alone Books
The Six Thousand: A Sci-Fi Thriller

Flurries Ending: A Thriller

Living with Men

Shades of Green: The Fraulein and the Handyman

From the Heart: A Lifetime of Poetry

Children's book
The Mitten Tree (Kindle only)

About the author

Kelly Young has lived all over the great province of Ontario, Canada.

A graduate of the English literature program at the University of Waterloo, she moved to a small town on the shores of Lake Huron in southwestern Ontario with her husband, and together they raised two sons and a clowder of cats. She has since retired to a small city in further south southwestern Ontario.

Kelly worked as a freelance reporter for many years, switching briefly to full-time reporting for a local paper before taking herself to a much quieter bookstore. After coaching two competitive swim teams, she worked at the municipal pool teaching people of all ages how to swim until her early retirement at age 55.

Kelly enjoys swimming, reading, and watching Star Trek in all of its different iterations. She is also an avid collector of dust and keeper of cats.

Follow her on Amazon, Facebook, Goodreads, Pinterest, LinkedIn, and Bookbub, request a digital autograph at Authorgraph, or visit her website at http://kyoung18.wixsite.com/kelly-young-author.

Manufactured by Amazon.ca
Bolton, ON

40441367R00159